❀ Created with Vellum

SHATTERED OAK

RENNEN'S ORIGIN STORY

THE MERGED SERIES

CLAUDIA BLOOD

DRAGON BANE PUBLISHING

This novella is from the **Fierce Hearts: A 2022 Charity Anthology of Romantic Fantasy & Fantasy Romance for Ukraine** and has only been reformatted and had some small edits from the anthology version.

A dryad snubbed by the forest must unite with a wolf cursed at birth to defeat the coming evil.

The evil infiltrating the world had not yet touched Rennin, but it wouldn't stay away for long. All hope rested upon the prophecy, one she believed was tied to Gant.

But when her relationship with Gant falls apart, Rennin meets a cursed werewolf who changes her entire view of the life she thought she knew. Rennin must accept her new reality and embrace her fate if she hopes to save the dryad...and herself.

Will she be able to overcome her past and fight against the darkness threatening their world? This is the origin story for Rennen and Adelram and a novella set in the Merged Series.

Fans of fantasy and adventure will be drawn in by the enchanting setting and the powerful emotions that drive the characters.

Trigger warning:
This book contains stalking, death, and self-defense that ends in death.

PROLOGUE: MEADOW

<u>Mid-morning, Primum tenth, 100 years post-Merge</u>

Meadow Deeproot did not expect the time with her daughter to end so quickly.

"You've stayed too long." The voice was barely a whisper and was the first time anyone from the hamlet had addressed her directly. Apparently, it took being hidden in their tree for the Dryads to be brave enough to speak to a Tree Protector.

Had they always been so timid of their kin or had the war outside their protected forest finally had an impact? The world outside grew more dangerous with each passing season. The danger was the only reason she and her mate had agreed to bring their daughter to the Dryads' forest.

Doubt twisted her gut and tightened the skin in her forehead. She could still change her mind and take her daughter back home with her. But back to what? The constant fear? The battles? The uncertainty? The safe haven for the army's children had fallen and only by blind luck had Rennen not been there. Meadow took a deep breath and loosened her hands which had fisted at the thought of losing her child. This was the last safe haven, a place that would allow Rennen to discover the beauty in the world. A chance to see something stable and good. A chance for her to develop her powers without the constant fear.

"I know." Meadow nodded. Resisting the call of her mate and her duty was growing more difficult with each day. She could feel the evil upon the land and she needed to do her part to aid the good.

The good needed all the help it could get. Otherwise, her mate would've come with her. But instead, he'd said his farewells from his commander's tent. The huskiness of his voice and the slight tremor of his hands had given away his feelings. The memory of him in pain closed her throat and reminded her of what was to come. She too would need to give her goodbyes. "I need to say goodbye."

Her stomach twisted. She was not ready to let go, but she must. Rennen must stay at the Hamlet because of the cursed boy born on the same day. Her gaze swept to the edge of the play area where the pale, dark-haired boy stood. Gant shuffled his feet like he wanted to run and hide, but his gaze was fixed on Rennen. She filled a bucket from the stream, oblivious to the unease around her.

"She must stay." The invisible speaker reminded Meadow.

A wisp of anger trickled into Meadow's body leaving her very aware of how different she was from the rest of the hamlet's docile citizens. To maintain balance, the Earth Mother had made Tree Protectors more passionate and more motivated to action because their main purpose was to rid the world of cursed Dryads. What better tool could the Earth Mother have chosen than a 'good' Dryad to fight a 'bad' Dryad? But nothing was ever that simple. Good and bad were just a series of choices and actions. And this moment was a pivotal choice for her daughter's future.

A squeal drew Meadow's attention back to her daughter. Rennen still held the bucket but now she stood behind a sopping wet little girl who darted into her tree. The other green-haired children slipped away, leaving Rennen alone. She would get used to being alone. Deep conflicted feelings twisted in Meadow's chest at the thought of Rennen experiencing the same loneliness Meadow had here. Loneliness was better than fear. Better than learning so young how fragile life was.

"B-but she said she needed to be watered." Rennen's words came out in a wail.

Meadow covered her mouth to keep from laughing and leaned closer to her old tree. No tree behind the veil that protected the hamlet would house a Dryad that embraced her fate and transformed fully into a Tree Protector. Still, she placed her head against the tree and hoped the tree might remember her.

The tree was silent. A tree outside the veil might allow her to stay for a night or more, but the tree would never be her home. She'd given up so much for what she believed in. And she would give up more. The sorrow ached with each breath, adding to the feeling of finality. She would have to leave her daughter today and go back to her mate.

"She is just like you were." The voice sounded faintly exasperated.

"Yes, she is." That loosened something in Meadow's chest. Growing up in the Hamlet would not be easy on Rennen, but she would survive. The other dryads would not understand her extra energy, drive to help, or how deeply she would feel. It wouldn't be long before they started to avoid Rennen. At least she would have a friend. Even if he was cursed, he should ease some of her loneliness.

"You were only trying to help." Gant was at Rennen's side and laid a hand on her shoulder.

"I was trying to save her." She sounded so confused and mournful. Meadow could not see her face but could imagine her lower lip sticking out and the pouty frown.

Gant wrapped Rennen in a hug. She wriggled out a moment later and scampered away into the underbrush. He followed after her.

"Could she be the one to lift the curse and merge the lines?" The voice sounded so hopeful.

But Meadow knew already, Rennen was not the chosen one. That spark between Rennen and Gant had gone only one direction. If the fates had been kind, the two would have had an instant bonding and given the good its first victory. If they'd had that victory, it might have been all the world needed to push back the invaders. If they could have defied the invaders, she might have been able to raise her daughter in peace with her mate.

But none of that was to be. She rubbed at the ache in her chest. If she told the truth, she could keep her daughter and bring her back to the front-lines of a losing war. If she hedged, Rennen would stay here and be far safer, but she would be without her family and would be barely understood or tolerated. Meadow's head ached at the no-win choice before her.

"Maybe." Meadow's chest felt as if it was cracking open. Hopefully, she'd made the right choice for her daughter and her future safety and happiness.

1

———

RENNEN

<u>Dawn, Luminous first, 150 years post-Merge</u>

The dawn brought no answers. The ritual had failed Rennen Deeproot.

Rennen stood while the others still lay in a spell torpor around their fairy ring. They slept peacefully, in piles of haphazardly strewn limbs.

Their quiet connection had always been just out of her reach. No matter what she'd done, she'd never really belonged. The ritual had been meant to heal her estrangement with her tree and then open that connection with the rest of the hamlet.

She rubbed her eyes. If she could rest in her tree that would reinvigorate her. Like all descendants from the tree protector line, she had an oak in the south end of the hamlet away from the normal clusters of trees. The normal Dryads.

The trickle of worry about whether her tree would still accept her seeped down her back, leaving a small chill. Her connection to her oak had been drifting away much like a fall leaf in a stream.

She left the fairy ring and walked along the footpath next to the creek. The creek with the round stones burbled happily, unaware of Rennen's worry. Her bitterness about that lack of connection still stung.

Her tree looked the same. The main trunk was broader than she could wrap her arms around, the first branch above her head was a place she'd loved to climb and hide from the world. She pressed her forehead to the ridged bark and waited for the tingle at the base of her spine that would serve as a greeting and allow her entry. She waited for some sign that she still belonged.

As the moments trickled away, the air felt heavier. Her breath caught in her throat. Even her tree, the one she'd lived in since she was little, had rejected her. But she wouldn't die. Oh, no, she was her mother's daughter after all. Tree protectors could live without trees.

She lifted her head from the tree and really looked at the place she could no longer call home.

Dappled sunlight played in the small glade where she'd first met other Dryads. The rest of the hamlet mothers had kept their children away from her and from one other family.

When she'd asked when she would get red hair like her mother, she'd been told that ancient magic had shattered her people and spawned the cursed, marking them with dark hair. Earth Mother had responded by forming the tree protectors. They looked like any other Dryad with green hair until they chose to fight.

Her gaze fell to the black elm that had once housed Gant. Her stomach twisted. He'd been the dark-haired child that day, more than willing to spar. They'd both been outcasts, who'd over the years become friends, then lovers.

The glass of the promise necklace was warm under her

fingertips. Gant had refused it each time they finished their love-making. He had refused her promise necklace on the day he'd left for Cursed Keep. Rennen had begged Gant for one last meeting. They were to meet today just after mid-morning.

Her stomach churned as if aphids had invaded her gut. This could be the last time she saw him unless she could get him to promise to her. She pushed away the idea that he'd refused time and again. That no amount of seduction on her part had made him want her bond.

"How could you choose darkness?" she asked the wind and the trees and Earth Mother.

The rustle and creaks of the trees gossiping above stopped at her voice. They seemed to wait to see what she would do. For a moment, she wondered the same thing. What could she do? She didn't want to be an outcast and abomination like her mother, but her options grew more limited with each passing season. Her fate had been sealed when she and Gant had been unable to form a love bond.

She shook herself, banishing those thoughts. She knew what she had to do. Today was her last chance to get Gant back from his curse. The last chance for her to live a normal life here in the hamlet. If she took the shortcut past Shattered Oak, she could be to the Cursed Keep before mid-morning. He should be waiting for her.

When she saw him, she would convince him to bond even if she had to seduce him again. Bonding would break their curses. Gant had been a good lover. Though, if she was honest with herself, it had been just a fun physical act, nothing deeper. And that was the problem. Maybe if she tried again, it would be different this time. It had to be.

She hurried along the sacred way. Gray trees stood as somber guards along the path. How long before they considered her an outsider?

With each step away from her hamlet, the tension in the air grew. The morning was unbroken by the hoot of the tawny owl. The normal bird chorus was strangely quiet. The squirrels, usually rustling in the leaves hunting for nuts, were hiding within their dens and hidey-holes. Perhaps there was a storm approaching. Although that explanation felt wrong and added a chill to the air.

The soft tinkle of glass in the breeze drew her from her thoughts. Shattered Oak stood in the clearing. The old matriarch towered above the slender adolescent trees like a storyteller surrounded by children.

The ragged, black scar branded by unbearable heat centuries ago had filled in over the years. This wound had caused the cursed to spawn. A splinter of evil lodged in their line. It was her ancestor saving the tree that caused the Earth Mother to notice and transform her into a Tree Protector.

Hanging from Shattered Oak's branches, thousands of the promise necklaces glittered in the sun. Each necklace had been placed there as a symbol of the couple's promise to be together. Rennen touched the promise necklace around her neck. The glass was smooth against her fingers.

She swallowed convulsively and leaned her forehead against the rough tree bark. The tree responded with a spark of recognition that started in her spine, "Seedling of the Dryad who saved me."

The tree's deep musky scent relaxed Rennen's shoulders and back. Perhaps she was not doomed. Perhaps her mission to Cursed Keep was not hopeless. Perhaps she was not cursed to become like her mother. Someone fated to fight and was able to kill. A dryad who survived without a tree.

"Have you found that thing you must fight for?" The rustling sigh of Shattered Oak's leaves punctuated the tree's question.

A shudder rippled through her body and her hopeful

thoughts fell away like leaves in the fall. The tree that was central to the Dryad people knew she was doomed.

Her hand slid down the jagged bark from as high as she could reach to the top of the roots in ritual farewell. Her fingers broke contact and the tree quivered.

She hurried through the forest and followed deer trails out of the Dryads' protected land. The cursed land started after a swath of barren field. Perhaps some ancient war had burned the trees so that the cursed folk might be watched. Or perhaps the healthy trees had slowly migrated away from the fouled land. Whatever the reason, a clear divide marked the land.

She waited; senses open for a hint of Gant's vibrations. His vibration had been solid but different from the rest of the Dryads. Darker, wilder. His connection to his tree was just as loose as her own.

His vibrational trail led her closer to the keep. Each step closer, her stomach twisted at the extra note of darkness that now pulsed through his vibration. Then she saw him, a hulking shadow waiting under an elm with drooping branches.

She crossed from healthy waving grass to dried, cracked ground and then to black-trunked trees with bark and leaves covered in fine white lines. The air had a tang of sickness and decay. She shivered but kept moving.

Gant stepped into the light.

She gasped and felt as if she had been flattened by a rush of wind. Had it been only a week since he'd left the hamlet? Like an overripe fruit left to rot, Gant's bruised, tattooed skin pulled tight over bone. Sunken, shadowed eyes bored into hers. They were darker and more menacing than she remembered.

A shiver of fear raced up her spine and lodged at the base of her skull. Leave. Leave now. He was already lost to the evil lodged in his soul. She shook her head, grabbed her courage, and stepped closer. No, he was her only hope. If they could merge the lines by love, they could fix the rift in the Dryads. She would not be doomed to kill. He would not be transformed into a monster.

His gaze met hers and the young man she had known all her life surfaced, pushing back the binding curse. The dark tattoos faded from his face.

"Bind with me to break the curse." She reached out to touch him.

"I cannot. You don't love me."

Rennen flinched at the truth in his words. She cared for him. All she had to do was say she loved him. He would believe her and bond with her. But when she opened her mouth to say it, nothing came out.

He caught and kissed her hand, bringing it to his cheek. "It is far too dangerous for you to be near the keep. You must leave me to my fate," he said, his voice a rough croak so different from the smooth tenor he'd once sung to her with.

She frowned and the forest darkened. "Don't you love me?"

Gant crouched so they were eye to eye and kissed her on the lips. The kiss was not a renewal of passion, but of goodbye. "That doesn't matter. The darkness has too great a hold on me. Our bond would be false. You would become as I am, a slave to the Master."

She stared into his eyes trying to decipher the emotion on his face. For a moment she saw it, he did love her. He loved her enough that he did not want her to suffer with him. He wanted her to be free. Her heart ached. There must be something wrong with her that she couldn't love him.

"You must go. The wolf will find you. Or worse yet the Master."

She shivered. He would not mention a normal forest wolf. This wolf must be one of the race of shifter folks. A feral, violent people. If the Master had made one his slave as he had with the cursed Dryads, he would have a powerful hunting dog. Her heart beat frantically. Only such a wolf was able to track a Dryad.

"I will go to Zinnia or another tree protector." She hugged herself and stepped closer to him. "They might help because of Mother."

Slowly the light faded from his expression and the shadows gathered. The magical tattoo wrapped around his face and neck like barbed wire. He would no longer meet her eyes. "I will become a monster. Tell the Tree Protector it is on my upper right arm."

"What is? Why would they care?" She did not want to think about what it meant.

"There is only one way to remove my curse now," he said this softly, his voice resigned.

Her stomach plummeted and tears pricked her eyes. A cursed Dryad would become an almost invulnerable monster. Only a Tree Protector might be able to kill him, and only if they knew the source of his brand. "I could—"

"No. It doesn't matter. Don't come back here again." He kissed her hand before releasing it and backed away slowly, reluctantly, as if he ripped himself in half with each step. The dark tattoos swirled to consume his face, neck, and arms, leaving only a pale trace of untouched skin near his ears.

This was it. The last time she would ever see him. Her last chance at being normal.

Her heart shattered like a tree struck by lightning. She dropped to her knees and moaned. "Don't leave me."

"I–" His mouth snapped shut, caging what else he might have said. He glanced deeper into the cursed woods. "Damn, the wolf is near. You must fly from here. If we are lucky, he will follow me."

2

———

ADELRAM

Adelram Dire lifted his nose and scented. The damp murky flavor of the forest held a subtle hint of jasmine and mint that reminded him of wholesome things.

Wholesome things that had no business being here in the cursed lands. The fur on his back lifted and his hand broke the branch he gripped. The leaf remnants drifted down from his perch with a rustling sigh. He must be mistaken; nothing good came here.

A crunch brought his attention to the main trail that twisted through the dark woods. Below him, Gant raced back toward the keep. There was nothing stealthy in his step. He acted as if he wanted Adelram to follow him and that woke Adelram's curiosity. He fought the urge to chase Gant.

Bond slaves did not leave their posts. Especially when they were first being conditioned. For Gant to make a noticeable return to his post meant one thing. He must want to be chased and he must be protecting something or someone.

The scent of lavender and mint teased his nose again, bringing a slow tightening in his gut. He hopped easily from tree to tree in his hybrid form, getting closer to the scent that did not belong. He spotted something at the edge of the cursed land.

A forest maid stood in shadow. Pale and straight as a birch tree. Something about her tugged at him. Dew clung to her green hair like the blades of grass he'd played with as a pup. This must be the wholesome thing.

She must be why Gant still resisted his Master and fought the darkness. Why he'd left his post. Why he'd tried to be a decoy. Had they been lovers?

The possibility that Gant held the heart of this maid sent a small curl of jealousy to Adelram's chest. He'd wanted a family once, until he realized the extent of his curse and had realized he would bring the downfall of his whole clan if he was not careful. Never that. That was why he'd left them.

But Gant had left this tree maid here at the edge of the cursed land, where any number of evil things might prey upon her. Including Adelram. Surely, Gant would not have done that if she belonged to him.

For the first time, Adelram allowed himself to want something. If this maid got away, she would need protection. Gant would eventually turn into one of the Master's creatures and she would be in danger. Not only from the Master but from Gant himself. That opened a path Adelram had never thought of.

The ice that encased Adelram's heart thawed just a little and the seed of hope settled with a painful stab. Perhaps if his mate was other than a Wolf, he could avoid his curse. Love was not a requirement to become mates after all. Need and respect could be enough.

Perhaps he didn't need to be an outcast and mateless till the end of his days to protect his clan. Perhaps he could go home. He took a deep breath to ease the tightness in his chest.

Adelram focused on the maid who had awoken this possibility. She must know something dangerous was near for she stood, barely breathing and poised as if to run. The predator in him wanted her to run. So he could chase.

Each passing moment, the urge to stalk forward itched along his back. How close could he get before she fled? He didn't want a weak potential mate. He wanted someone strong and worthy, even if she was not of the clan. And even if he'd never love her.

He set his claws into the tree so he could shift and shimmy silently to the ground, but in that instant, he was off-balance, she turned and sped out of the cursed woods. Something glittering fell to the ground where she'd stood.

At last. Fierce joy set his heart racing ahead of his feet. Stealth no longer needed, he crashed to the ground and bounded after her. Her scent locked in. He'd be able to track her anywhere. She was his, if he wanted her.

When he reached the edge of the cursed land, she was already across the field and in the woods beyond. She was fast, good. Perhaps she would be worthy.

He followed the faint hint of her trail. She must have tried to mask her scent in the water. No water would ever mask her scent. The mint and jasmine scent wafted up into a tree where she tried to lose him in the treetops.

A soft imprint of a big toe on a riverbank. The thread of green hair caught in the brush. Each step he took brought him closer to her, but she maintained a lead. She *was* strong, a worthy potential mate. The need to claim her burned through his veins.

Her trail stopped twisting through the trees and arrowed north. The woods gave way to gently rolling hills. The black spikes in the distance caused the first trickle of worry to raise the hairs on his back.

As he raced ahead, the black glass of Mount Venua clawed up from the horizon. It was the only remains of an ancient wizarding duel. While there should be no remaining wizard-born creatures, the land itself had a strange reputation. What was she up to?

Black specks glinted on the hill. Her scent veered to a faint trail he might have missed. He slowed his pace but followed still. The black specks were shards of glass that would've shredded his paws. She was tricky. Even better.

The scents around him changed, adding a strange undertone to the normal tree perfume. Unease skittered down his back and caused him to stop. His gut said he was in danger if he did not figure out the scent puzzle.

A faint tinkling to his left brought his gaze to a small tree. Deep emerald leaves waved at him in the breeze. The sense of oddness was increased by the stiffness of the leaf and something that looked like ice on the stem.

Before he could reach to touch the ice that could survive in spring, a small blue bird fluttered near and landed on the tree's branch. The bird seemed to have no idea Adelram was nearby. It fluffed its feathers and teetered on the branch, blinking its eyes at him as if the bird were drunk. How odd.

The bird could make a quick snack. He leaned closer until the smell of feathers and that strange sweet undertone filled his senses. The bird allowed him far closer than a healthy bird ever would. He hesitated to snatch it. Something was wrong.

The bird shrieked, and wildly, flapped its wings. Adelram fell back with a yelp. The branch bent, but the bird's feet remained stuck to the branch. The bird's distressed calls lessened as the ice from the branch flowed around the bird slowly encasing it in a transparent trap.

He shook his head. The air on the ground was clear of that odd note. The scent must be disorienting to birds as well as wolves.

She'd led him into a trap. The realization made him want her more, not less. But first, he would have to catch her. He stood, careful to avoid the trees, picked up her scent, and followed.

Despite the danger, his steps felt light as he followed her scent. He might even be grinning at the challenge she threw his way. He continued toward the mountain through this treacherous terrain. This was the most fun he'd had since he was little. Before his curse got in the way of his life.

Slabs of black glass cut upward and reflected patterns of puffy white clouds that looked like sheep grazing on black grass. Her scent led to a sandy path that twisted through a crack in the mountain.

He stooped to enter. His steps caused the glass to hiss, sending a chill down his spine. The glass pinched above him. The walls crowded in and the light fled. Though it was dark, he could tell that she was just ahead. Her mint and jasmine scent was out of place in this dark recess.

A sharp crack echoed in the small, enclosed space between mountains, and shards of glass rained down ahead. He paused; his desire tempered by concern. This was not a place for a living creature. The walls were too sharp. The darkness was too complete. If he followed her farther in, he might force her into taking chances she would not normally take. She'd already proven herself. There was no need for her to be injured.

If he did not chase her now, he would have to lie in wait, but there could be more than one exit from the mountain. If he was serious about this maid, he needed to catch her and bring her to his clan before night fell. But, she may not move until nightfall. He wouldn't if he were her.

He bit his lip. If the Master found out from Gant that

another Dryad had been on his lands, they'd send out a hunting party to nab her. They probably would not notice Adelram was missing for a few days. He sighed deeply. There were too many ifs.

Waiting was too risky; he needed to catch her and do it soon so he could bring her to his clan.

That decided, he resumed stalking her, transforming to his smaller human form. With each step, the walls closed in and the cave narrowed, leaving barely enough room for him to get through if he hunched over, and then it constricted smaller than he could pass. He braced his hands to push, but drew them back with a hiss. The sharp glass had cut his hand. The sunlight sparkled just out of his reach. She was on the other side where he could not follow.

Warmth danced in his chest. She'd tricked him again. She truly was a worthy foe. He scented to see if she'd stayed by the door and smelled something metallic mixed with her scent. Blood. His stomach dropped, and his heart jumped.

Red drops were splattered across the sand at the exit. He crawled forward on his belly until he could go no farther. He twisted and extended his arm so he could dip his finger into the blood. But he knew before he brought it to his nose. It was her blood.

His intended mate was hurt. He howled in rage and sent the birds aflutter on the other side of the crack. He growled and snapped. Blocked for now, but he would find her.

3
———

RENNEN

Dawn, Luminous first, 150 years post-Merge

Rennen knelt at the edge of a pool hidden by the long branches and silver-green leaves of a willow. Her heart had finally settled after the wolf's long howl. She was no expert on wolves' howls, but his had sounded frustrated, on the edge of anger. Which mirrored how she was feeling. If the howl had a touch of sadness, fear, and a wrench of pain at being rejected it would have reflected her current state perfectly.

He'd stay frustrated. The tunnel she'd come through was the only shortcut across Mount Venua. It would take him a day to get around the mountain. She'd have plenty of time to get away.

Trailing her hand in the icy water, her blood swirled with the movement. She was injured. Not fatally so, but enough to slow her down. She had no tree to heal her. No people to seek protection from, but she was not without resources.

She twisted to touch the tree to ask for assistance, but liquid fire played along her ribs. Wincing, she drew in a sharp breath and parted the leaves of her shirt to look at her ribs. The glass had scraped her deep, leaving red gouges and a black sliver poked from just beneath her bottom rib. She plucked the sliver out quickly and it fell from her shaking hand.

She pressed her hand onto the tree. The tree's bark parted under her fingers and pink inner bark bubbled to the surface, thickening into a deep pink paste. She brought the paste to her mouth and cringed at the bitter taste. The tree's bark would help, but she needed to clean her wounds.

She splashed cold water, cleaning the wound the best she could. It was not perfect, but it would have to do until she found safety. If the hamlet wasn't possible, should she go to her mother or maybe a tree protector?

Her mother traveled with her human bond mate. She could be anywhere. Zinnia, another tree protector, lived to the west on the other side of the valley. She was not known for her compassion, but she might be willing to shelter Rennen until she could come up with a plan. Tree Protectors could create magical weapons with tree branches and their own blood. Maybe Zinnia could create something that could reconnect Rennen with her tree and her hamlet.

She stood and walked along the path, extending her senses to the forest. The area was safe. The trees and birds responded with bits of gossip sent in flashes of images. The trail meandered the way she wanted to go and she moved as quickly as she dared, her feeling that time was running out hovered over her. It made her move a little more quickly than she should. The ache in her ribs grew. The willow's healing gift faded as time passed.

She would need to rest and find another willow tree. A small glade with a patch of grass warmed by a pool of golden sunlight looked inviting. She sat against the oak tree and rested her head against the tree's trunk. Her side ached and now that she was not distracted by the forest gossip, her own troubles tried to burst to the surface of her mind.

The image of Gant's twisted face caused a shiver to crawl down her back. They were both lost because she was not able to love him. Maybe she couldn't love. That unhappy thought was interrupted by the warning croak of a black crow.

The crow flapped into the glade and jumped to a branch near her head. The bird cawed again and tilted its head. She reached out and the bird returned an image of a wolf. The wolf was bigger than normal and had a pattern on its fur different than a forest wolf.

Her heart thundered. She shot to her feet. Could he have found her so soon? Her hand fluttered to her mouth. What could she do? Her hand hurt, her side hurt, her heart hurt. Maybe this was it. Maybe it was her fate to be caught and be killed the same day her heart died.

A gray bird darted to her left. With a worm in her beak, the bird fed the chicks in her nest. The babies peeped and opened their mouths wide. She remembered how excited she'd been when she saw her first bird family. The awe that an egg could transform into a bird and someday fly. How hopeful she'd felt for the future. Was she really ready to give up?

No, while there was life there was hope.

She sprang in the direction of Zinnia's home, but something lurked in the shadows ahead.

The wolf paced forward. His dark fur receded as he transformed into his human form. He stalked toward her with sinewy grace. His black hair reminded her of Gant. Her heart twisted at the thought. Leaves and twigs stuck at odd angles in his hair as if he had bullied his way through any and all obstacles to get here, and he panted heavily as if he'd run the whole time. His bright blue eyes looked ferocious and stared so hard that she skidded to a halt.

Their gazes locked. She swallowed; her mouth suddenly dry. He would pounce at any moment and end this game.

He leapt across the space that separated them and grabbed her wrist in a firm but delicate grip. She froze in shock, expecting teeth, not his gentle touch.

He leaned into her space and sniffed her side and hand. His eyes flashed and a low growl rumbled from his chest. He sounded angry, but not exactly at her. His actions made no sense. She searched his face looking for clues. His gaze softened and he took her uninjured hand gently in his own. Her heart fluttered in confusion. She pulled her hand away. He released her hand but tightened his grip on her wrist.

Panic flooded her veins; she was a hare caught in a snare. Trapped. She dug her toes in the mud and pulled, but he did not move. He merely watched her, his face a still pool that didn't betray what he was thinking. She clawed at his hand to remove it from her wrist.

"I'm not going to hurt you." His voice sounded like an ancient gate creaking open after years of neglect.

Her mouth opened wide enough to catch moths. Wolves did not talk to prey.

A gentle stroke of his fingertip closed her mouth. Fear receded and left her light-headed. She almost laughed at the absurdity. Next thing she'd see a tree pull out its roots and walk away. She shook her head to clear the image. If he wanted to hurt her he could have, but what if he was just playing with her? Like a cat might play with a chipmunk. "What do you want?"

"Come with me." He tugged her arm. She resisted, feeling his vibrations. They were wild, like a forest creature. There was darkness, but it didn't have the same feel as Gant's. It felt more like hunger than true darkness. Hunger did not ease her worry.

"Why?" She wrestled the worry down and kept her voice even and soft. Wild things did not respond well to loud noises. If she had any hope of escape, she'd need to lull him into lowering his guard.

He met her gaze, seeming to search her face. "You look tired. I know a place where you could rest safely."

He kept surprising her. His hand tightened briefly on her wrist and then released some pressure. She shook her head and pushed at his hand. "I have a place."

"I can guard you." He seemed to want to say more, but he closed his mouth and continued to gaze at her. The wolf that chased her from the Cursed Keep suddenly wanted to guard her. She huffed out a laugh.

"From your Master?"

He sighed. "He's not my Master."

She raised a brow and watched his face, wanting to ask him why he was at the cursed keep, but resisted. His reason for being there didn't matter.

"Not. My. Master." He said it slowly, firmly. Each syllable was hard and clipped.

"And that makes you trustworthy?"

His eyes narrowed and he leaned in. Emotions flashed across his face too quickly to read, except for the exasperated anger his expression landed on. "I could just carry you where I wanted." His words felt like a threat. She cast a quick look at his chest and arms. He probably could carry her. That made the decision for her. She needed to be on the ground to get away, not trapped in his arms.

"Take me to Blaze Woods." That was where Zinnia lived. All she needed was a moment free and a willing tree and she could evade him. She pushed away the thought that finding a tree would be hard. It took an act of will to connect now. Once he let her go, she'd make a run for it. She would wait until they were almost to Zinnia and then she would make her escape. She'd save her energy. If he was willing to guard her to the woods, that would let her rest.

He blinked and seemed to consider her words. "That is on the other side of clan lands. What if we stop in clan lands and then I will take you to the woods?"

Even though his words were soft and coaxing, there was something not quite right. Some hidden meaning she was just not understanding. It was the subtle pause at the word 'then'. Like he had no intention of letting her leave once on clan lands or like something would happen on their lands that would change everything. There was a tension in his face as if a lot hinged on her response, as if he wanted her to come of her own free will.

Rennen took a deep breath and her side throbbed. The light-headed feeling persisted. The forest she wanted to get to was still so far away. She needed to focus her dwindling energy on figuring out how to get away from the wolf. Going to his clan lands was foolhardy. What choice did she have? She'd be surrounded by not just one but an extended pack of the blood-thirsty monsters. So, she had to time her escape.

He squeezed her wrist lightly, breaking into her thoughts. She'd go with him, but as soon as she was close to Blaze Woods, she would make a bid for freedom and find Zinnia.

"We have an agreement?"

"Only if you don't carry me." She had to be on the ground if she had any hope of escape.

He inclined his head in agreement, hiding the flash of some-thing on his face. "You should let me tend to your wounds."

She flinched and through gritted teeth said, "No need." She didn't want him to touch her any more than he already was.

He looked about to argue, but just shook his head. "This way."

4

———

ADELRAM

<u>Dawn, Luminous first, 150 years post-Merge</u>

Adelram winced every time the maid's breath huffed out. She was so stubborn. Her face seeded with pain, grew lines and furrows as its harvest. Her arm cradled her side. She tripped on exposed roots and stumbled along the trail. He resisted the urge to pick her up and carry her. When she had fallen by the shallow pond, he'd offered. When she'd paused so long with her forehead pressed against an oak, he'd cajoled. But she'd refused and reminded him of their agreement. So now when she stumbled, instead of offering to carry her he put an arm around her to steady her. For as long as she'd let him.

They did have an agreement and he wanted her to keep her end. He just needed to start the process of binding with her and hopefully, the rest would work out. He'd never seen a Maid out of a tree for so long. He'd only ever caught glimpses. Even as her energy flagged, every attempt to carry her or look at her wound was evaded.

He held her wrist carefully. Her pulse was still much higher than it ought to be. Step by step, he brought her closer to his clan's land. Now all he had to do was get the clan to accept the mating. No one else had a non-wolf mate. Such a thing had happened in their history but had to be approved by the Elders.

When he crossed the border, his shoulders relaxed. Clan land. The outer guards would pick up their scent soon. He threw his head back and opened his throat with a series of yips and then belted out a long howl that deepened at the end. The guards knew now he was here with another non-wolf and planned to go straight to the elders. The guards responded, adding their notes to his song. He was free to pass.

The maid jerked at the first note and pulled away from him. Her eyes were wild.

"Shhh. All is well." He kept his tone low and gentle and used the same tone he would soothe a scared pup. If she struggled too wildly, she would hurt herself more. When he stroked her arm, she gazed at him blankly for a moment before calming. She didn't seem to be completely aware of her surroundings as if she was hoarding her energy.

He took the left fork in the path and headed to the sacred glen. The glen didn't look like anything special until he stepped into it. Only then his non-magic sight could see the power that radiated from the ground. It even smelled magical, like summer lightning. The hairs on his back stood. At the center, he knelt next to her and waited to see if the clan would honor his request.

Moments later, the shadows under the trees thickened. The air grew colder. Five pairs of golden eyes circled. They blinked in and out of view. The elders were here. A large wolf with a white muzzle and paws, gray body, and a black tip on his tail loped from the trees. Adelram knew him only as the Eldest. He favored one leg just enough to give an odd hopping gait. The gold had faded from his eyes leaving them a milky blue. He approached them.

The maid grabbed a branch and slammed the Eldest as he approached. He flew back into the brush.

Adelram held his breath, this could be the spark and spirit that would cause the clan to honor his request. They did not want weak members of the pack.

The rest of the elders howled in amusement.

She shivered and backed into Adelram. The warmth of her back pressed against his stomach. He did not want to notice how soft she was. Or how womanly and warm she felt against him. He certainly did not want to give her any reason to move.

The Eldest rose. The fur slid back into his skin, the claws and fangs shrank leaving a wrinkled old man crouched before them. The folds on his face twisted into a grin. "You are in the mating circle. Adelram requests a mating." The vegetation thrummed at the deep note. Adelram's heart picked up. The pack would allow the mating.

"T-to me?" Her gaze bounced to his. Her eyes were wide and startled, her lips parted, and she tried to step away. She must think him a monster.

The elder chuckled a series of yips. "The clan is bound to protect you regardless of what you choose."

"Why?" She sounded so unsure, so hesitant, his stomach tightened in sympathy.

"Will you accept his suit?" The eldest circled and marked the ground with his foot. Digging deep with bare toes and then he lifted his foot to add a delicate line with his big toenail.

"If I do?"

"You will be mated."

"And if I don't?"

The Eldest shrugged as if it was not important. "He will be killed."

Even though Adelram knew the code, his heart stuttered hearing it said aloud. Mating was a risky business. It was permanent one way or the other.

She jerked in Adelram's grasp. "K-killed? For nothing more than bringing me here?"

Adelram felt a flush of warmth in his chest. She did already care for him, at least a little.

"Eldest, my lady is wounded." He'd seen the wince when she moved too quickly.

The Eldest tipped his head toward the maid. "May I?"

She bit her lip and then nodded.

The Eldest pushed apart her shirt to expose her wounded side. A swift calculated expression crossed his face. "I could heal you if I had a wand."

Adelram glanced between them. Where were they going to get a wand?

She stared at the Eldest for a long moment and lifted the branch in her bloody hand and murmured something that sounded like the wind in the trees rustling the leaves. The branch shimmered, the blood, nubs, and twigs melted into the base, and it straightened. A pattern of leaves and stems, and sun and moonlight swirled around the outside.

His breath caught. He caught the Eldest's gaze, realizing that this maid might be more than a Dryad. When he looked back, the glow had faded around the wand. She looked dazed and drained, her face pale, an arm drooped listlessly at her side. The wand clutched to her chest.

The Eldest bowed with hands raised palms up to accept the gift. She placed the wand in his shaking hands. A bright flash of light flared and thunder boomed through the clearing.

The Eldest hummed his approval. He flipped the wand up, caught it in one hand, and pointed it at Adelram. "This is going to hurt her."

Adelram shuddered. He'd experienced the pain that came from magical healing. The healing worked better if you could stand still through the pain. That had been easier to do when someone had held him. This service was the least he could do for the possibility of having her as a mate.

"The healing will work better if I hold you still." Adelram brought the wrist he held across the front of her body to her shoulder. His other hand snuck under her other arm which lifted it up. He held her firmly in his arms.

She trembled but did not pull away. "I understand."

The Eldest stabbed the wand into her wound. The air shimmered with magic like sand sparkling in the sun on a hot summer day.

She jerked and moaned, but Adelram held her firmly. His stomach twisted. He hated her feeling pain. He told himself that it was necessary. He closed his eyes and pressed against her wishing he could take her pain. The smell of burnt flesh hung heavy in the air. The golden light flared brighter and then died.

Sweat dripped down her neck and she shuddered. The heaving rubbed her back against him. He felt every tremor. Every shake. He held her close and gave what comfort he could. She sagged against him.

The Eldest cleared his throat and his gaze fixed on the maid. "Since you did not deny the bond, the first part is now placed. You have three days to accept his suit. Do you understand?"

Adelram had thought her passed out, but she flinched in his arms and raised her gaze to his. Alarm, dismay, and fear flashed across her face. She must still fear him. She swallowed and nodded. The energy seemed to leave her in a rush, her body went limp in his arms.

Adelram picked her up and cradled her against his chest. Her hair fell like silk across his shoulder. Now that the mating focus faded, he cringed. A spirit of the forest would not think much of his clan or his den. Could he convince her to accept his bond? Would being mated to someone not in the clan confound the dark curse that haunted him?

31

5

RENNEN

<u>Dawn, Luminous first, 150 years post-Merge</u>

Rennen stretched and the stroke of fur down her torso told her she was naked. She felt so strange. At peace and perhaps even safe. She did not want to move but relished the feeling. The vibrations were strange like she was in the middle of a flock of birds. Or a colony of ants.

Or a pack of wolves.

Wolves. Memories poured down like a waterfall, Gant, the chase, the Eldest, the wand. Her peace broken, her heart awoke in a panic, trying to escape her body. Did she dare open her eyes?

"You don't have to pretend to be asleep, my lady." A gruff voice said far too near for comfort.

Her eyes flew open. Adelram, the old wolf had called him. Adelram sat next to the bed. He'd been so close and she'd still felt safe. "Adelram, where am I?"

When he grinned, his eyes widened and his whole face softened, the grin of a child delighted by a surprise. "You, my lady, are in my den."

She swept her gaze across the walls. Rounded dirt walls and floor made her feel at home. A natural feeling space with the bed she was on in the middle of the room. On the left, wild, chaotic, red, blue, purple, and yellow splashed across the walls. A frenetic sunrise. Maybe he was more than a beast. She met his gaze, wondering who he was.

"Why do you call me my lady?" That seemed the safest of questions.

He bit his lip and looked down. "I don't know your name." His voice was soft and hesitant. He glanced up and looked almost hopeful.

The ludicrousness of her situation hit. She snorted. Once, twice, and then fell back in helpless laughter. Her life hadn't gone as planned. She was supposed to be the chosen one to reunite her people. Instead, she was banished from her home and in a Wolves' village. When she was done, she said mostly to herself, "Pre-mated, and my mate has no idea my name."

His mouth opened as if to say something but nothing came out. He tried three times before he shrugged and turned his red face away. He cleared his throat. "Hungry?"

She sat up and the blankets slid to her waist before she could grab them. Cold air smoothed from her shoulders to the top of her breasts. Dryads went naked for many occasions, but alone in a wolf's den, her nakedness felt different and dangerous.

A gasp had her looking over at him. A strange expression crossed his face. He stood quickly and whatever was on his lap clattered to the floor. A pile of cloth landed on her lap before he bolted out of the room. "Come out when you are dressed," he called over his shoulder as he left. She'd think his response amusing if it were not for the strange pull in her chest at the look on his face.

Rennen closed her hand on a simple leather short sleeved-shirt and tie-around skirt. Fur trimmed the bottom of the skirt. Fur was not her first choice for clothing. She would almost prefer to be naked, but his reaction to seeing just her bare shoulders and breasts made her want to put on more clothing, not less. His expression had been covetous and wild and had confirmed the dangerous feeling coiled deep in her core. Not an expression a male had cast in her direction before. Some small part of her liked it, but the rest wondered if that was his beast showing.

She slid the shirt over her head and when she smoothed it down, felt her bare throat. Her bond necklace was gone.

Her heart stuttered and her hands shook. She searched the bed. Gone. If her bond necklace went missing she could never mate. Panic stabbed through her system. She was not ready to give up having her mating recognized by her people. Not yet.

She crawled on her hands and knees. Her hand swept under the bed and found nothing. She shook the blankets off the bed, but still, there was no sign of her necklace. She sagged back. The Dryads only recognized a mating with the necklace. Even her mother with her human mate had put their sacrifice on the Shattered Oak.

Rennen had no way to bond with Adelram, even if she wanted to. Not for real. But if she did not mate him the way his people mated, he would die. She pushed away the guilt. She'd led him into traps when he'd chased her. How was this choice different?

Blaze Woods was nearby. She could still get to Zinnia and get back some semblance of her old life. Maybe she could find her necklace. Or find a replacement. Did it matter? A bond necklace should only be used for love and she didn't seem to be able to love. Her head ached with conflicting options. There was no clear path.

When finished dressing, she walked out into the bright sunlight. Adelram leaned against the wall outside the door. His relaxed pose looked as if he could stand there all day. Like he was used to waiting. His gaze scanned the area, drawing her attention to the wolf village laid out in the valley. A sliver of dread pricked her back. She was in danger, soon to be surrounded by monsters.

Silver smoke rose from a large central mound. Three circles made of smaller mounds had what looked like neat-rowed gardens growing on the tops.

"Wolves have gardens?" She didn't mean to sound so surprised, but she hadn't known wolves had gardens.

"Go up and see." He gestured to a ladder affixed to his hut.

Rennen climbed up. His garden was a tangled mess speckled with trilliums and violets. Carrots, onions, squash, and other edible plants fought for space against the weeds. It seemed to have been left to run wild on the top of his mound, but she knew if managed right, the space could feed a family.

A black bird darted down to the village. The elevation made it obvious that Adelram's mound was not in an outer ring. It was off to itself away from everyone else. A small bit of sympathy tightened her gut at the thought of him being an outcast even amongst predators.

When she came down from the garden, his face seemed harder, shaking her from her soft thoughts. This was not the time for sympathy. She needed to get to Zinnia.

"When can we go to Blaze woods?" She didn't miss the flinch her words caused.

"Let's get some food first." He did not quite meet her eyes.

"I'm not hungry."

"You need to eat after a magical healing." His voice was firm. He was right, she could feel the rumble in her gut. She needed to eat. Being low on fuel was not wise. Especially while she was in enemy territory.

He took her hand and led her to the village. What would a whole village of monsters be like? She braced herself for anything. As they wound their way between the houses, she waited for something to happen.

Just as they entered the village and rounded a corner between two dens, a movement near her feet caught her attention. A small black wolf hunched ready to spring at something around the next corner. The pup wiggled its butt and tail. She could almost feel the pup's excitement. Then the pup launched itself and a moment later a startled yelp sounded.

"Mommmm," A high, young boy's voice called.

Rennen broke Adelram's hold and peered around the corner. The wolf pup tugged on the hair of a small hairy, brown-haired boy sprawled on the dirt.

"Lydia get off your brother and go take your Pa some water." A small woman in hybrid form, a fuzzy human with extended fangs, sat cross-legged on a nearby mound. She had materials to make a basket laid out around her and the shell of a basket was started in her lap. Her hands had not paused in weaving as she scolded her daughter.

A snitch sounded from the roof of the house behind her. A large hairy man dug in the garden roof. The shovel moved in an easy rhythm. The black pup slunk to the well where she transformed into a dirty young girl. She dipped the dipper into the well and went up the ladder where she presented the cup to her Pa.

The man paused and ruffled the girl's hair as he took the cup. "Thanks."

The girl grinned at her Pa and then turned her gaze to stare at Rennen.

Rennen realized she had stopped and had been staring at the family. Heat razed her face. She tensed, waiting for an attack.

"Adelram." The man nodded at him.

"Patrick." Adelram nodded back.

The two kids slipped back to wolf form and crept closer, and sniffed at her feet. She backed into Adelram's hard chest.

"They are but curious." His warm breath tickled her ear, making her gasp. She nodded and let the pups sniff her fingers and legs.

"You should scratch their backs," Adelram said. She glanced at the parents who smiled with no teeth which made her feel oddly disarmed.

The little girl was the first to pounce on Rennen's foot. She reached into the pup's thick fur and gave a good scratch. The pup arched under her fingers and then rolled over tummy in the air legs splayed. The little boy meanwhile rubbed against her leg. She stroked his chin and jaw. The girl pup made growly noises while she rubbed her back on the ground. Rennen chuckled. The boy pup bumped her hand which had stopped moving. She gave him another good rub. He bumped again, but his sister chose the moment to pounce on his back. They bounded away, yipping and pouncing.

They were just like the kids in her hamlet. That thought occupied her as they went deeper into the village. Wolves in full furs and in partial fur talked, laughed, and worked. They didn't seem to notice her at all. Didn't seem to consider her prey. At least not yet.

A few more steps brought them to the large central mound. It was tall enough to cast shadows between it and the next mound. Stone stairs on either side of the entrance led to the garden above. Gray stones arched above the entrance and more stone formed stairs into the mound. She glanced at Adelram who just smiled in return. Taking a deep breath, she stepped in.

The ceiling glowed a pale yellow, reminding her of sunshine. Rows of wooden tables and chairs lined the walls and at the far end, a gray haired woman stirred a boiling pot. The lady ladled stew into bowls on the table in front of her. This scene was not what she'd expected at all. It was peaceful and cooperative.

While she was occupied looking around, Adelram picked up two bowls and gestured to a table. The bowl was heaped with bits of meat and potatoes. Her stomach lurched and she pushed the bowl away.

"You should eat."

"I can't eat that." Her voice sounded horrified to her own ear.

He took her bowl and wolfed down her portion. "We can go to the garden."

He finished the last of his portion and licked his lips. There was nothing wrong with what he did, it just made her wonder what his lips might taste like. Her heart sped and a tingle started low between her legs. What was wrong with her? She needed Gant, not this Wolf. Heat crawled up her neck and face.

He smiled, a slow easy smile that said he knew about her tingle. His eyes wide and hopeful started a chain reaction in her body. Everything felt more intense and the air heavier. Sensations like the brush of fur trim on her thigh, the vibrations of ten different warm bodies in the kitchen flooded her awareness.

"What did you do to me?" Her voice sounded low and strangled.

A loud scrape broke the silence between them. A giant red-haired male perked up and scented the air. He stood and stepped closer, towering over her. She shrank toward Adelram who growled low and menacing. He batted the reaching hand away and shoved the other man's shoulder.

Red snarled back and circled to bypass Adelram.

But Adelram stayed in front of Rennen and matched how

Red circled, never once backing down or taking his eyes off him.

"She's mine." Adelram lashed out his hand now tipped with six-inch claws. He raked them across Red's shoulder and drew blood.

Red snarled but backed away slowly.

The smell of fresh blood sent the room spinning. Rennen needed to get away before she was tainted by the violence and the blood. It was the spilling of blood that caused the final irreversible step on the path of Dryad to Tree Protector. It was what her mother, and everyone from her line, had done to earn their red hair. Rennen would not be like her mother. A dryad who killed and kept killing as part of her human mate's army. No, she would never be like her mother. The urge to flee rose and would not be denied.

Rennen stumbled up the stone stairs and pushed past a knot of wolves. Everyone oriented on her frantic first steps out of the hall. Her gut plunged. This was no time for panic. Not in the middle of a village of predators. Their ears twitched and noses sniffed. They shifted toward her as if drawn by her wake. She had to calm down or risk one of the wolves attacking her. A deep breath did nothing to calm her, but she slowed her steps anyway. She needed a place to hide, the garden was the best option.

She climbed up the stairs to the garden with slow measured steps. Being surrounded by greenery helped, but her heart still thudded. When she looked down from her perch in any direction, a wolf stared up at her. She was no closer to being free. For a moment, she wondered where Adelram was. He would've been able to handle any unwanted attention. He would have protected her. She shook her head, casting the thought away, she didn't want his protection.

She moved to the center of the garden and crouched so no one could see her. The plants were strong here. They were willing to gift her power. She carefully collected wisps of energy, being sure not to harm the plants, but spread out the request across the garden. When she had enough, she focused the energy on her hand making it tingle. The tingle intensified until the skin shimmered and took on a transparent leafy pattern. The tingle spread up her arm and the camouflage followed. She stood.

Zinnia was to the west which was also the side away from the mound's entrance. If she moved slowly, she might be able to get to the edge of the village undetected. Or at least without being stopped. She slid down the side of the mound. The nearest wolves shifted and sniffed the air, but did not seem to see her. So, she walked past them, keeping her distance.

A few puzzled looks and slow sniffs followed her progress through the village, but no one stopped her. Hopefully, she would be free of the village before Adelram caught her. Then she would not need his protection and could resist her growing attraction to him. All she needed was to make it to Zinnia's land.

6

———

ADELRAM

<u>Dawn, Luminous first, 150 years post-Merge</u>

Adelram heard his lady leave, but had to keep his gaze on Finnegan. He'd backed down across the room, but had yet to look away. Until he accepted Adelram as the winner by looking away, Finnegan would remain a threat to his lady. There would be others, of that Adelram was sure, but he'd take on any challenge. Finnegan finally dropped his gaze

Just as Adelram began to relax, a heavy hand gripped his shoulder. Another challenge. He turned, claws out and ready to attack. The rangy thin man stepped back, his hands up and eyes downcast. It took Adelram a moment to recognize Seamus through the red haze. He wore an acolyte sash. Adelram shook his head and gulped in a deep breath. Not a challenge, but possibly something worse.

"The Elders wish to speak with you." Seamus' message made Adelram's stomach drop. The tree maid would never choose him if he didn't have time to lay out the advantages of such a mating.

She would not need to worry about him getting physical with her. That couldn't happen. She would never love him and he was afraid of what he might do after his primitive response to her partial nakedness. She'd already run from him after he'd smiled at her. Better to have a chaste mating than be rejected. But if the Elders kept him too long, he would lose his chance. Maybe they were doing this on purpose. Maybe they wanted him to fail as punishment for the curse he would bring to the clan. He was destined to cage the pack and for that, he would deserve to die.

"Do you know why they want me?"

Seamus shrugged and led the way silently. They walked across the village and most importantly, away from his lady's scent, to the ceremony hut. The air thickened as he left the bright sunny day and walked down the stairs into the hut. Sage-tinged smoke hung in the air. He'd been exposed to it enough that he knew the Sage was for keeping evil spirits away. He used to worry the smoke would crumble him to dust but that had never happened. Five of the six elders formed a line between Adelram and the fire. They were each in full ceremonial garb: brightly colored masks, necklaces of strung fangs, and red sashes.

"Adelram, why have you returned to us?" The elder in the red, scaled mask stepped forward and shook his rattle as he talked.

"I brought a potential mate." He kept his voice even, despite the panic at losing his time with her.

The elder wearing the green feather mask lit the smudge stick, wafting the fumes around Adelram while chanting. The elder wearing a smooth white mask pulled a rope and a small door popped open on the wall. Drawings of watchful wolves surrounded the hole. The hole meant to let out the bad spirits and not allow them back in. The air shifted making the chimes tinkle in the breeze.

"Is that the real reason?" The rattle punctuated his words.

That confused Adelram. What other reason would he have for coming back? "Yes."

The green masked elder chanted and circled closer, the smoke from the smudge stick twisting through the room making it seem like they were in a cloud.

"Drink this." The elder in the furry black mask held out a cup.

Adelram downed the drink in a single gulp. The musky, bitterness was no longer a surprise. The concoction worked its magic, easing away his anger and making him want to talk. He slid down to the mats on the floor. Someone turned him so he could gaze at the crossing branches on the ceiling. The edges of the world softened.

"Tell us about this mate."

The question surprised Adelram even in his hazy state. What did he know about her? She was smart and fast. The run across the mountain had proved that. She was compassionate and did not trust him. She had secrets and was not what she seemed. Not fragile and not innocent, but strong and savvy. And he was very physically attracted to her. He realized at that moment that he already had a bond with her. He hadn't had a bond in so long he barely recognized the beginning of one. And the fact that he wanted it there, was unexpected.

"Why do you resist her bond?" The elder seemed to know his thoughts. The rattle shook.

"It has to be chaste." The thought of not exploring her body twisted his gut. The thought of not bringing her pleasure made him feel dejected. A mate should take care of any needs she may have. He should protect and cherish and satisfy.

The silence deepened around him. He waited for the questions he knew were coming. About his time in the cursed keep. About the Master. About his mother.

"Will you not ask about the Master?" He broke the silence to ask. It seemed vital to ask.

"It is important that you embrace who you are."

Cursed and broken and a danger to the clan echoed through his head.

The red masked elder stopped shaking the rattle for a beat and looked at the white-masked elder holding the door open. Even though they had on masks, the look felt odd, not censorious, but instead filled with dismay or surprise. Almost as if they could hear what was in his heart and Adelram could feel their thoughts as well.

"Eat this." The white-masked elder helped him to sit and put a root in his hand. "You need to eat it all."

The root smelled pungent and bitter. After the first bite, a warmth spread to his lips and gums. He chewed as if it were a stick. Gnawing on it and finding it strangely satisfying. A tingle at the tips of his fingers coursed energy through his body. The lethargy that had gripped him was replaced with a burst of energy.

Adelram's attention focused on the black-masked elder who until this point had not spoken. Even though Adelram could not see his face, something about the way he moved reminded him of his fading memory of his mother. "You need to protect your mate."

The elder's words sent a flood of possessiveness into Adelram. Suddenly he realized his lady had been going to Blaze Woods to the red-haired tree maid. The one that decimated all that went in, good or bad. The thought that his mate might be in danger cracked something in his heart.

Adelram needed to protect her. It was as vital as breathing.

He scented the air and found the faintest hint of her scent. He would always be able to find her.

Shifting to wolf form, he ran. The red-haired tree maid protected his clan on the north, killing anything that dared to set foot on her land. She was said to have no friends, but the trees and the swords she carried. The shiver that slunk up his back said if he didn't stop her from entering Blaze Woods, he would have no bond to worry about. He had a mate to protect.

7

———

RENNEN

<u>Dawn, Luminous first, 150 years post-Merge</u>

Once outside the edge of the village, Rennen picked up speed. The greenery swayed as she passed. If she could make it out undetected, she had a real shot at getting to Zinnia's forest. Hopefully, Zinnia would help her.

"Leaving so soon?" The voice cut through her thoughts.

She skidded to a halt and whirled toward that deep voice. The Eldest knelt in human form. His bare fingers dug a hole in the black dirt.

"How did you see me?"

He lifted the wand she'd given him in answer. Her heart shuddered. The wand she'd created for him. One more step down the path of being a tree protector. She waited for him to throw accusations at her, but instead, he turned away and resettled his basket. He sat so calmly that his presence calmed her. She was not being chased, not being judged. She could stay or go if she wished to. Her worries and her fear, all faded into the

46

background and curiosity won out. She stepped near. "What are you doing?"

He handed her a thin green plant with dirt that still clung to its roots. The plant was alive with the potential to be something more. More of the same plants lay in his basket.

"I grow these from special seeds in my garden." A long line of the limp plants extended in each direction. He planted the last one that connected the two sides. "They are for protection. The Dark Master will come."

"Because of me?" The idea of putting those cute pups in jeopardy tightened her gut.

"In part. But that is Adelram's story to tell." He was not looking at her, but at the row of plants.

It made no sense that Adelram had brought her here. Not if she was putting them all in danger.

"Want to help?" The wand glowed and he made a sewing motion. The new plant wove into the line of plants causing a chain reaction. Each plant lifted and wove into its neighbor. Like they would form a net around the village. But it didn't seem very strong. These weak and ineffectual plants could not possibly protect the village. A village she'd put in additional danger with her presence. She gave in to the urge to help.

Rennen tucked the loose plant in her pocket and reached out to read the spell. Since it was her wand, she could feel the magic. A protection spell, like what a tree maid might put around a favorite tree or watering hole. Protection was something she understood. Her hand on the ground, she found the pattern and then expanded by asking if the trees and the brush would help. The willing ones she wrapped in the Eldest's casting. The grass brought them together, the Eldest, the trees, and Rennen.

And then something more happened with the rush of wind and tinkling bells. Those limp plants drew the magic inside and the magic spawned creating a magical flash that connected them.

She knew the Eldest. His real name was Virgil. He came from a tribe far, far away. He needed to protect his people from the growing darkness of the Dark Master. He knew she had her great, great grandmother's nose. He knew dark secrets that she only glimpsed in the rush of his life. Secrets he would protect with his life.

She knew the lives of each tree and plant who were now a part of the bond. From when they first tasted the sun, to every break and bug bite and mating.

And at that moment, they knew her as well. They knew her deepest secrets and darkest corner. They knew about her mistakes with Gant and her growing attraction to Adelram. They knew about her mother. About her need to belong and desire to be the one that merged back the Dryad lines by mating Gant. About how lost and alone she felt when she could not love him and had no tree and therefore no home.

And they accepted her with no reservations. For the first time, she found a place where she belonged. She could be a part of this village. Her mistakes would not matter.

The Eldest leaned in and patted her leg. His sympathy caused her heart to pound, her throat to close. The past rejections rose and taunted her. Who was she to enjoy such acceptance? If her chosen had left her and her mother chose to be a Tree Protector, rejecting her in the process, she couldn't be worthy of belonging.

She rejected the bond the spell offered and drew away. Her heart galloped. She needed to get to Blaze Woods and out of this confusing world of gentle, protective predators.

Rennen leapt up and sped past trees to the west towards the foothills, trying to outrun the confusion. What was wrong with her? This was becoming a pattern. Would this be her life? Constantly fleeing?

She crossed the stream in a single bound. When her feet touched the ground on the other side, she knew she was in Zinnia's land. The land itself was branded with her signature.

Zinnia, the tree protector with the surliest reputation. She never left her land, and killed trespassers like a frog would eat flies. Rennen needed a way to approach her, but she could not stop to think. She crested the hill and smacked into a warm body sending the body flying. Red hair swirled in the air. The red hair of a Tree Protector.

Rennen tumbled and landed with a crunch on dry leaves.

Zinnia landed hard against a tree. Then she bounced back up and drew a curved sword. "Who dares enter my domain?"

Rennen stood slowly and brushed the leaves off to avoid looking at Zinnia. "I am sorry, sister. I did not know where else to go."

"Why do I smell wolf?" Zinnia sniffed strongly and brought her nose to the vee of Rennen's neck. She held still, not yet sensing any anger or danger.

"It's been a long and confusing day." Her voice sounded so small, so defeated, so sad.

Zinnia tilted Rennen's chin and stared at her face. "I know you."

Rennen towered above Zinnia, but Zinnia's energy and leather armor made her seem much bigger. Zinnia's sharp cheekbones reminded Rennen of Gant. Zinnia's hair had appeared red at first, but a dark cast under the red made it look more purple. Rennen searched her memory for any trace of this woman. There was nothing. "I don't know you."

"And yet I know you." The sword slid away into its sheath. Zinnia put her hand out palm up. The other hand fisted onto her cocked hip. Her green eyes flashed in challenge making a chill crawl down Rennen's back. Tree Protectors had uncanny abilities. There were rumors that some could see into your soul. Rennen hesitated.

"You would refuse me a reading?" Zinnia said in a soft hiss. The tops of the nearby trees rattled together like clashing sabers.

Rennen bit her lip and then slowly put her hand palm up on Zinnia's palm. Red hair tickled Rennen's wrist as Zinnia traced the lines of Rennen's palm. She muttered and frowned and then shook her head.

"Come with me, sister." Zinnia dropped her hand and headed deeper into the woods.

Rennen struggled to keep up, she'd not had a chance to recharge. The trials of the past days leadened her limbs and slowed her steps. Sleep had been good, but what she really needed was some food and a place to truly recharge.

A moment later, the heart of Zinnia's forest opened. The oldest tree in the forest towered before Rennen. Five people could link arms and still not encompass the girth of this ancient oak. She could feel its power through the ground, thrumming up her legs. The oak was not perfectly symmetrical but had a large white rock the size of a standing man embedded in its side. Her heart went out to the tree. Something monumental had happened here and it was of the same magnitude as Shattered Oak. Despite the warmth of the breeze that tickled her arms, something deeper felt cold.

Concentric circles of white stones filled with protective power that snapped and crackled girded the big tree. Outside the largest circle, young oaks and other trees competed for the light, but inside, just grass and flowers grew. The rocks and trees must be protecting something.

Zinnia leaned against the oak and patted it. "Do you know what this is?"

Unsure what Zinnia meant, Rennen answered, "An oak?"

"Next to the oak." Zinnia gestured to the stones.

"Some stones." She felt stupid, and heat filled her face.

Zinnia glanced up sharply and examined Rennen's face. Zinnia must have seen something amusing because she tilted her head back and laughed until she fell, wrapping her arms around the tree. The oak swayed its branches and rustled its leaves in amusement. The tree was far more aware than Rennen had seen any other tree.

Once she got herself under control, Zinnia asked, "Do you know what a tree protector does?"

"Kills." The whisper passed the lump in Rennen's throat.

"No. We defend and protect." Zinnia nodded once, an abrupt motion, her gaze fierce.

"But your hair is red, you've spilled lifeblood." Rennen wanted to take the words back. It was not wise to poke. Zinnia had something more than red hair.

"I have." Her chin came up, the sheen of tears flashed before being blinked away.

Rennen hadn't expected Zinnia to admit her sins. She did not look embarrassed. She looked determined with her jutting chin and firm lips.

"Y-you don't deny it."

"How could I? There are certain things worth fighting for. Worth protecting."

"But–"

Zinnia made a cutting motion with her arm. "No, listen."

Rennen's mouth snapped shut under Zinnia's imperious gaze. "These rocks are the top layer of a tomb. The tomb of one who should not be named. More evil than the Dark Master could ever hope to be. He shattered more trees and broke more lives than anyone in living memory. I ensure he stays in his tomb."

Zinnia's words rolled around in her head. Rennen was

missing something. "How did that make you a tree protector?"

Zinnia stepped away from the old oak and circled Rennen like a wolf stalking a fawn. The forest darkened. "Why didn't you and Gant leave the woods together before the curse struck?" The word felt like daggers striking Rennen's chest.

"Th-there was no time." A lie. He had wanted to. She realized the truth; she had not wanted to and he'd stayed for her.

"Truly?" Zinnia lifted a taunting brow. "Or was he not the thing you were meant to fight for?"

Rennen opened her mouth to say that she did love him, but could not. Her heart thumped faster at the truth. She had not loved him enough and was not willing to give up her hamlet to be with him. Heat flooded her chest, neck, and face. Shame crawled into her heart.

"You are a Tree Protector. It is who you are. He was cursed. Why were you together?" The statement hung between them in the air. Zinnia demanded an answer with her silence. Even the wind seemed to pause to see what Rennen would say.

"I thought I could fix our people. If only I could get him to love me." The words were small and soft in the silence.

"You thought you were the chosen one?"

"Yes." The confession was barely audible over her own pounding heart.

"And did you get him to love you?"

"Yes." Of that, she was sure.

Zinnia watched her face again. "But you did not love him."

Rennen closed her eyes and swallowed the hurt those words caused. Maybe she was broken and not able to love since she was a Tree Protector.

"Tree Protectors are made to love," Zinna said as if she knew what Rennen was thinking. "In fact, they feel more deeply than a normal Dryad."

Rennen didn't know what to say to that. How could those that kill be more prone to love?

"What you are meant to protect will stalk you." Something sad and bemused flickered across Zinnia's face. Her lips softened and a half-smile played on her lips which reminded Rennen of Adelram's smile when she'd used his name for the first time.

"That person will mix you up. And you'll do things you never thought you could or wanted to do." Zinnia's unfocused gaze made Rennen believe that Zinnia was not talking about Rennen but of Zinnia herself.

Rennen got an image of the wand she'd crafted. She'd known how when the Eldest had asked. Uneasiness flickered to life. If she were a Tree Protector, she'd given him a powerful talisman. And she'd given Adelram the start of a mate bond.

Rennen pressed her lips together and shook her head. She was here for a reason. "Can you use your wand to allow me back into the hamlet?" It came out sounding desperate and breathy.

Zinnia's face twisted with pity and something sad flickered across her face. "I have no wand. You would have to make your own and dip it in your blood."

"And that would get me back into the Hamlet?" She could still get the wand back from the Eldest, but it would mean he could not renew the protections on the clan's borders. Could she do that? Leave them unprotected?

"No, sister. You need to embrace the truth. You are what you are. A tree protector." Again, Zinnia's fierceness surfaced, flushing her face and making her eyes snap.

"But-"

"Tree Protectors make such a wand as a weapon. A weapon made to kill a cursed one."

"Are they always lost? The cursed ones?" Gant had been kind

to her and had been her constant companion. Did he deserve to die? Had she made things worse for him?

"Most are lost. A few over the millennium were strong enough to resist the darkness. We all have choices." Zinnia's fingers strayed to caress a strange locket on a chain tight around her throat.

"What happens when they are lost?" She'd been selfish, she realized that now. Gant had been left to suffer because of her choices.

Zinnia closed her eyes and gave a secret smile that was part grimace. "It's like being overrun by ants. They dig through and find everything useful and then change it to suit their purposes. Unless you can get rid of the ants, the ground is forever changed. And once it is changed nothing else can live there but ants."

"How could you know?" Rennen asked. Her words seemed too personal as if Zinnia had experienced them.

Zinnia said nothing.

The thought of Gant being devoured by ants had Rennen stepping back. A crunch drew her eyes down to the Tannin leaves. Some dryads changed these tough leaves into sturdy boots. Was she just like the leaves, unwittingly shaped by the forces around her? A helpless mix of options swirled in her head. She could try and rescue Gant, but he did not wish to be rescued because she did not love him. She could stay with the Wolves, but then what? Embrace the bond not only with the protective spell but with Adelram? She did not have a bond necklace, so it would not be a true bond.

"The wolf is on his way. If you wish to avoid him, you can go through my lands." Zinnia offered no hint of her opinion. Her expression was blank and her eyes clear.

"He will just follow me." He would follow her to the ends of the world. The thought eased something deep inside. Maybe that was an option.

"If he enters my land, I will rid you of him." The words were precise and cold.

Rennen's stomach twisted at the thought of Zinnia killing Adelram. She didn't want him dead. If she let Zinnia do what she intended, then Rennen would be responsible for the downfall of two men. The first through her selfishness, the second through inaction. If she let Zinnia or even his own kin kill Adelram, what did that say about her?

Zinnia's gaze connected with Rennen's gaze. "The more important question for you is what will you do?"

8

——————

ADELRAM

<u>Dawn, Luminous first, 150 years post-Merge</u>

In his haste, Adelram almost missed the tree maid. She leaned against a tree at the edge of Blaze Woods. Almost as if she were waiting for him. He skidded to a halt, panting and uncertain. He hadn't had to chase her. What did it mean? Her expression gave him no clues. She did not smell of fear and did not seem to be in any danger. She was waiting to meet him. Something shifted in him. This could be his chance to win her over.

"My name is Rennen." Her words were soft and hesitant and brought a warmth to his chest.

Adelram shifted to his human form and sat near her. He tried to quell the rising hope. It was a good sign that she had finally given him her name. "Thank you."

"Why were you at the cursed keep? Are you cursed?" she asked quickly as if she were afraid of the answers.

He flinched and scrambled to come up with a different topic.

Talking about the keep would not help with his goal. "I saw a tree maid out of her tree once. Then she disappeared. Do tree maids really go inside trees?"

She blinked at him and looked uncertain, tilting her head to the side. "Most Dryads must merge with their trees to live."

"How long do they merge?"

She shrugged and ran her hand along the tree's trunk. "It can be years. Some won't come out for a hundred years."

Amazement distracted him. "Why would they disappear for years?"

"One was ill and sleeping in her tree helped her feel better. One was too far from her tree for too long and had to repair the damage. I even know one who did it because she was avoiding a suitor who pursued too closely." She shrugged as if it was normal.

He felt a pang of worry. She could disappear. "What's being inside a tree like?"

She seemed to hesitate and then gazed at the tree above her, and sighed. "It's like sleeping in a nice warm bed surrounded by something that loves you." Her face looked so sad, her mouth pulled down, and a hint of moisture sparkled in her eyes. He realized she must miss her tree. How soon before she had to go back to her tree and leave him?

What would it be like to sleep in love? What a strange idea. He knew about protection but love was another matter. "Aren't they vulnerable?"

"Most Dryads live within the Veil which is protected against attack. The ones outside of the Veil use protective magic and hide. Much like your clan."

He grimaced. "My people do many things to try and protect themselves."

"Is there a reason you are avoiding talking about the cursed lands?" She sounded curious.

His stomach dropped and he swallowed against the bitterness in his throat. "Nothing good goes there." He tried to make the statement sound final. He had no idea what he was doing. What was he thinking about wooing a tree maid? He could not even woo one of his own.

"You are not evil."

That simple statement stopped the monologue of self-doubt. He cleared his throat. "How do you know that?" His voice sounded gruff and strange even to his own ears.

"Dryad's can sense that." Her tone was contemplative like the words were for herself more than him. Like she had just realized something she hadn't known before. He got the feeling that she was looking at him with more than her eyes.

"How?"

She frowned, looked away, and bit her lip. "Dryads can." There was something about the words that seemed so sad. "At least I-I can."

He wanted to ask what she saw when she looked at him, but the words would not pass his lips. They were clamped shut, and a strange feeling skittered up his back. He couldn't look at her face. Her verdict would be written across her face in the way her eyebrows raised in horror, the way her mouth pulled down into a frown. Maybe she would step away and slowly retreat to not awaken the beast within him. His heart pounded and he fisted his hands. He didn't want her to think of him as evil. He didn't want to be evil.

Her fingertips touched his shoulder and he flinched at the contact. "Are you well?"

He lifted his gaze and saw her face was full of soft curiosity and he let out a laugh that held no humor. She needed to know the truth.

"When I was born, the elders did a casting as they always do. This one was dark. Upon the bond, the end of the way, the end of life, the wolf folk in a cage of their own making." Dread settled in the pit of his stomach as he waited for her face to change. He waited for the disgust to color her expression and for the idea of being mated with him to drive her away.

"What does it mean?" A faint line grew between her eyes.

"I have never felt even a hint of a bond before." Even as the words left his mouth he wondered if it was still true. The elders had shown him that he had a bond with her already. A slight and fragile thing that might not survive the beast that he was. He glanced up at her face, which still looked puzzled. He allowed a flush of hope to warm him.

"And that is odd?" The line deepened and the corners of her mouth tugged down.

"For my people. They connect with each other with different levels of bonds." If one was not in a pack it was hard to explain what it was like. Maybe a relevant example. "Do you know why they kill in a failed mate bond?"

"No."

"I would not be able to stay away. I would not be able to help wanting... To be by you. To smell you. To hear the way you breathe. I would kill anyone who hurt you." He swallowed hard. "The mate bond is jealous. I would not be able to let you be with anyone else. Just me. Forever me." He could not meet her gaze. He hadn't meant to say any of that, but the drink from the elders still flowed through his system.

Her breath caught. He resisted the urge to look at her. Could this go any worse? He was wrecking his chance. He swallowed down the bitter taste which rolled in his gut.

She cleared her throat. "My mother is a warrior and fights in a human army with her lover."

That was not what he expected her to say. He looked up in surprise. She was not quite looking at him and she'd caught her bottom lip in her teeth as if she had confessed something quite shocking. But her confession didn't seem wrong to him. Wolves joined human armies to help keep back the darkness.

She peeked up at him from under her lashes and glanced away. That glimpse of her expression made him think that she was waiting for him to judge her. He let out a breath he hadn't known he was holding. Maybe what he had confessed didn't seem wrong to her.

"And that is odd?" He quirked his mouth as an invitation to share in the joke.

"For my people. Life in all forms is sacred." She smiled at him hesitantly.

"What do you do when hungry?" He was curious. It was the order of things that everything might get eaten. There were plenty of things that would eat his kin and they, in turn, ate the bounty the world provided.

"What?"

"How do you eat if everything is sacred?"

She glanced away, but the corners of her mouth twitched upward. "To murder is to become a Tree Protector, an outcast. Shouldn't you be more upset about my mother?"

"Even if I cared about that, and I don't, why would your mother's choice affect what I might feel for you?" Her expression cleared for a moment and she met his gaze and grinned. It was a shy smile that made her eyes sparkle.

"Is a cage so bad?" Her voice was soft and hesitant.

His warm feeling evaporated and left behind ice. Wolves did not belong in cages. "Wolf folk descend into madness in a cage." His words snapped out before he could catch them. The drug still churned in his system, making him sensitive to his failures.

She flinched.

"I will be the one that curses them. The one responsible for putting the whole clan in a cage." He fisted his hands and hunched his shoulders, drawing back and walking away from her. Away from the sting of her words.

"Don't go that way." She grabbed his arm and jerked him back from the edge of the woods.

"Why?" He took a deep breath to calm himself. She hadn't meant any slight with her words.

"Zinnia will kill you if you enter her land."

The words stunned him. "Is that why you were waiting?" She could have been free, but she'd chosen to save him. That was reason to hope.

She nodded but looked away. The small pop of hope dissipated, replaced by a sinking feeling in his chest.

"Are you saying you're agreeing to be my mate?" He should be excited, but something about her body language was off. She did not want him dead, but not wanting him dead and wanting to be his mate were worlds apart.

"The clan will no longer want you dead." She rubbed her face and gazed everywhere but his eyes. "Is there an oak near the village? I need to rest a bit."

He nodded, waiting for her to say something more, but she turned and headed back toward the village. The silence was strange and heavy. Even the woods they walked through were eerily silent. He watched the way she held herself and tried to puzzle out what was wrong. Something was bothering her and it had to do with him. Maybe she was planning on hiding in her tree for a hundred years, like the dryad she'd mentioned. But the mating bond would not complete and he would die.

He showed her the old oak on the edge of town. She ran her hand along the bark and put her forehead on the tree. She shimmered and merged into the tree like she had walked through a door he could not see.

He sat with his back against the oak and thought about Rennen's words. He had a sense that she was saying more than what he thought. Or that what she was saying meant something different to her than it did to him. The urge to protect her was still fierce. But he was missing a part of the whole. So, he worried, like he might worry a stick with his teeth if he were in wolf form. Nothing quite fit.

"Did she offer her bond necklace?" The deep voice sounded from his right.

"What?" Adelram jerked his head up. The Eldest was at his side.

"A mating is not real to a Dryad without it." Adelram focused his gaze on the Eldest. Pity softened the old man's features.

Her throat had been bare. The freckle at the base of her throat would have been covered if she'd had a necklace. "She has no necklace."

"It would be a small bottle that glitters in the light."

Adelram froze. There had been a small glittery object where he had landed when he'd jumped from the tree and started chasing Rennen.

He shook his head. She'd never actually said she would mate him. Just that the clan would no longer want him dead. Now it made sense, she would mate him in the ways of his people, but it would mean nothing to her. They would not really be mated in her mind. Adelram's heart sank.

The mating would keep him alive. It would give him everything he'd thought he wanted. Could he accept a mating in which she would not be committed to him? One in which she would eventually leave him and maybe leave his clan open to his curse?

No, not only could he not put the clan at risk, but he wanted more. If she was not interested in a full bond with him, then he could not accept the mating. He closed his eyes and slumped against the tree. The dream of having a family with her and images of the quiet moments they would've spent together fell into the pit that opened in his gut, leaving him empty. She would never love him. He would have to die.

She'd been so sad when she'd looked at Gant and grabbed her necklace. It had clearly meant a great deal to her. Returning her necklace would be his parting gift. He would find her necklace and return it to her, before letting the clan take care of their failed mating.

A howling screech vibrated the tree. Rennen flinched, feeling the noise in her teeth. It grew in volume until she fell out of the tree, forcefully ejected.

The Eldest stood nearby. "You can move into Adelram's hut when you wish." His voice was cold and even. He turned and walked away from her.

She levered herself up and closed her eyes against the dizziness. "Wait, where's Adelram?"

He stopped and glanced back. "Cursed keep." His words were clipped and angry.

The dizziness eased, but not the confusion. "He can't go there. They will kill him. Won't they?"

The Eldest grunted. "Probably. He is going to reject the mating anyway."

The floor dropped out from under her. A swell of hurt lodged in her throat. "Why? He would rather die than mate with me?"

The eldest narrowed his eyes, but his mouth softened. "He would rather die than put his clan at risk with a fake mating with you."

The phrase fake mating made her flinch. Her feelings did not feel fake. They were small, just starting to sprout, but they were real. Without the bond necklace, the mating would not be recognized by the Dryads but that wouldn't make it any less real to her.

The Eldest's head came up and he looked sharply to the east. "He's been captured. I need to go prepare the protections. The Cursed tend to attack after a sacrifice."

The thought of Adelram in trouble sped her heart. He couldn't die before they had a chance at a relationship. The only strong tie she'd had was with her tree in the hamlet. Even that she'd known deep down was temporary. His bond would be permanent. It would be real. It would bring her the acceptance she'd always wanted. She had to do something to save the possibility of having a true mate.

9

____

RENNEN

<u>Dawn, Luminous first, 150 years post-Merge</u>

R ennen strode to the double-door of the cursed keep, panting from the long run. An iron portcullis' sharp fangs lifted high and ready to crash down. Blood and scorch marks splattered the red wooden door. The gray stones of the keep towered above her with an icing of lizard-bird shit. Hundreds of lizard-birds snapped and hissed at each other. A cacophony of screeches and clanks echoed from the walls.

She stood at the door, hands on her hips. "I challenge your champion for the life of Adelram of the Clan."

Nothing happened. The people in the castle ignored her. Waited for her to run away. No, it would not end this way with her ignored and on the run.

She put her hands on the door, a tree's corpse. A Fire-Pine ripped from its home in the far western mountains and dragged here to protect this evil. The natural fire of the tree still smoldered deep within the heart of the door. She fed it a tiny amount of power and reached for its ghost.

Burn.

The wood heated under her hand until she drew back with a hiss. The blood boiled off the door and black smoke billowed out from cracks in the wood.

The lizard-birds fell silent. The only sound now was the crack of the fire from the heart of the door and the hiss of water escaping.

She stepped back a few paces and the door burst into orange flames. They licked up, blackened the stones, and sent up waves of heat toward the lizard-birds. The air filled with the pungent scent of burning shit.

In a few moments, the door crumpled and left a pile of ash and an empty space between the walls.

When she entered, twisted shadows swarmed around her. They did not touch her but followed as she walked through the courtyard and to the next set of doors.

The doors opened to the arena.

She stepped into a large square room with a dirt floor. Eight-foot walls topped with rows of seats filled with cursed knights in dark full-plate armor. In the center, a simple stone tower dominated the space.

Adelram, bloody and chained, slumped against the column.

Dread rested in her gut. She straightened her back to resist its crushing force. Was she too late? Was he still alive?

A gong shook the room. "The Master is here," a deep voice said.

The knights all stood. A skinny man in a blue silk robe strutted to a jeweled throne on the balcony above her and sat. The knights sat as soon as the Master did.

"I challenge your champion for the life of Adelram of the Clan." She raised her voice to reach the Master and met his gaze.

He reached into a bowl with long delicate fingers and plucked out a slug. He dropped the slug into his upturned mouth and slurped it down with a smack of his lips. Tossing his long, golden hair off of his shoulder, he leaned back and snapped his fingers. The naked man next to him knelt on all fours, and the Master lifted his slippered feet to rest on the man's back.

"If you can beat my champion then you and yours may go free." The words resonated with deep power at odds with his frail frame.

For one heart-stopping moment, all Rennen could think about was Gant. Her fingers crept up to where her bond necklace should have been. She could still save him and make up for her selfishness. She could still learn to love him and save him and unite her people. She could do it; she could be the chosen one. That was all she'd ever wanted.

Adelram groaned, causing her heart to twist. But if she did that, where did that leave Adelram and his clan? She already felt more for him than she'd ever felt for Gant. She rushed to his side. When his gaze landed on her face, his eyes widened.

"You shouldn't be here." His voice was hard and clipped, yet Rennen thought she heard a note of vulnerability.

"Neither should you."

His face remained closed.

"I came because you were in trouble." It was a soft confession that seemed to crack the wall he had built. His face softened and he looked uncertain with his furrowed brow and lip caught in his teeth. Wincing, he tried to sit up straighter, but the chains prevented much movement. His shirt fell open and her bond necklace glittered at his neck. He must have found it here in the cursed lands. The significance of that action sped her heart.

A gate creaked open. She stood and stepped forward. There was no time to think about what Adelram having her necklace meant. A bulky figure filled the doorway, blocking the flickering torchlight from the room beyond. He ducked to exit the doorway and the barbs on his armor screed across the lintel. His vibrations seemed familiar and sent a trickle of unease to her gut. The door slammed shut with a dull thud.

"I present our champion." The Master's voice held a taunting note.

The champion removed his helmet.

Gant.

Gant, their champion. Gant, the fighter. Gant, her x-lover. Stone-faced, his gaze coldly assessed her, then flickered behind her to Adelram. His face grew even more distant and his vibrations even darker.

Her Gant no longer.

She raised her chin. The dread in her gut doubled, sticking her feet to the floor.

Gant closed the space between them almost as if he could fly. She dodged out of the way, but Gant must have had a different target in mind because he charged past her without pausing. He streaked to the center column and raised his sword. A chill swept up her body. Adelram would be unable to defend himself against such a blow. Her heart stopped and then pounded. The air froze in her lungs. Gant could not miss Adelram's chained body.

Tinkling bells filled her head, the magic of the Clan and forest rose up and surrounded Adelram with a magic shield. The sword bounced off with a shower of sparks.

Gant screamed and hacked at Adelram again and again. Gant swung and swung, anger and hatred twisting his face.

On one of the thrusts, Rennen saw the small tattoo between the thorns on his upper right arm. The curse burn, a small mark that looked like nothing more important than a small mole, but the dark tattoos swirled in and out of it. Just where Gant confessed it would be. The one weak spot on a cursed Dryad, but only with a tree protector's wand. She'd given her wand to the Eldest so he could protect the clan. She wasn't sure if she could create another and even if she could, she had nothing to make a wand with.

Gant oriented towards her. His face twisted and his lip curled up revealing elongated fangs. "You betrayed me."

"You chose the curse over me," she said, her tone even and soothing. Maybe she could talk to the man who'd been her friend.

He snarled. "I loved you, but you left me alone to die, and went off with your lover."

It was not the truth, but the stab of his words made her ache for what might have been if only she'd been able to love him. "He is not my lover." She backed away one step at a time to the wall, drawing Gant away from Adelram.

Gant's muscles tensed. Then he leapt at her and knocked her to the ground with the flat of his blade.

She twisted, but not quickly enough. The downward thrust of his blade sliced her arm leaving a trail of blood. The pain would come later.

She scrabbled out of the way. Heart pounding, she gathered her powers to defend herself, but nothing came at her call.

"Are you blocked, little one?" He crooned.

She reached out for any plant life, but the dirt floor offered her nothing. Dodging back, she touched the wall. Nothing. Some dark spell clung to the stone like mold and prevented her from reaching any plant life on the other side. She did not have much power left in her. Her short time in the oak tree had not restored her.

"I still love you." His voice rasped like rocks scraping together.

She still did not love him. Not that way. His face writhed

with a black mass of tattoos. He held the sword wet with her blood loosely in his left hand. The boy she'd shared so much with was gone. She mourned the loss of her friend.

"We have another option to be together." Gant watched her face expectantly.

"What are you talking about?" There must be something. Anything that she could use.

"You could join me. Here. Willingly take on the curse and we could be together again. You would love me then."

She staggered back and leaned against the wall. Could that be true? Could she love him if she took on the curse? Could she save her people, if she became a monster? If she willingly chose to become like her mother. Able to kill. Thoughts whirled in her head like a dust devil in the fall. Her body shook and she gasped for breath like the room was filled with water and not air.

"Take down the shield around your lover. Prove to me you want me. Just me." Gant's voice was soft and persuasive, the voice he'd used on her many times in their past mostly when he'd made trouble.

The shield. Everything stopped. She had not put up the shield. The Eldest's protection spell had. That was her link to some plant power. But how had the shield gone up? Her heart thundered in her ears as she traced the magic back to her pocket.

The small plant from the protection spell. Her hand slid inside her pocket and touched the grass from the Eldest. Even with that brief touch, she could feel the incomplete bond waiting for her.

There was another option, embrace the fight but on the side of good. Her mother was not just fighting with her lover, she was fighting against those who would burn the forest without thought. Her mother had given up everything to lend her aid to that cause. To give her bond necklace to that human. To the person she loved. To be willing to kill for what she knew was right.

A weight lifted and her gut unclenched. Rennen had found what was worth protecting. Adelram and his kin. She was not the chosen one, but she could still do her part to help the forces of good.

Rennen pushed down the fear and accepted the bond the grass offered.

She felt a click and a hum as power trickled into the thin reed of grass. The grass thickened and stiffened in her pocket and transformed into the wand she had given the Eldest. The only weapon that could kill the cursed. She had to do it.

She had to kill her childhood friend.

She needed an opening. Gant shook out his arm and the spines clacked together. Were they spines from a plant?

She took a deep breath and let it out and smiled. It was the best she could do at pretending to accept his offer. She walked forward and touched his armor and slowly raised her eyes. It was from a plant. She coaxed the thorns apart so she could thrust the wand into his arm.

"I cannot follow you into darkness." Her voice came out firm and even and sad.

His eyes widened and he pushed her away. "What?"

She stumbled back but stayed upright. "I am not willing to pay your price. You could still come with me, leave the curse behind."

Gant blinked at her for a moment, his eyes wide and his jaw loose. Then his eyes narrowed and he tightened his grip on his sword. He charged her, but instead of stepping back, she stepped forward. She slammed the wand between the thorns into his cursed tattoo.

A howl burst from the throats of the watching knights.

The thorns scraped her as she let go of the wand and dodged away.

He fell forward in slow motion. The howl faded. The cracking of the thorns as he hit the ground was the only sound in the arena. He was like a great tree toppled. The stick protruded from his arm and smoldered. A dark shadow fled up from his body and with it, the thorns melted away. His vibrations cleared of the dark influence and he was left alone and naked on the floor. Her heart twisted.

Rennen scrambled to Gant and put his head on her lap. She stroked his hair back from his now pale face. His eyes fluttered open.

"I'm sorry." Tears filled his eyes.

She closed her eyes and put her forehead to his. Her own tears combined with his. Her heart grieved for all they might have been.

"I should have chosen you over darkness."

"It is done now. You are free."

"Will you wait for me in the next life?" Gant asked.

"I cannot."

He nodded–a quick jerk of his head. "Perhaps we will meet again."

"Perhaps." She held him until he took his last breath and then closed his eyes and crossed his arms over his chest. She pulled the wand out of his still smoking wound.

Then the pain hit, her body arched as electricity pummeled her. The empty hollow place past grief recognized that she had embraced her destiny. No longer a tree maid. She belonged with Adelram and his kin. When the pain left, she still stood and gripped the wand.

"I have defeated your champion. I will take what is mine." Her voice rang fierce and true through the arena.

"This is not over." The Master waved his hand and Gant caught fire.

A small shudder rippled up her spine. Gant would have his next life and that empty shell held no value, but her heart still mourned him. She backed away to where Adelram lay. The shield no longer protected him. With a touch of her wand, the cuffs opened and she helped him to his feet, and avoided looking in his eyes. His eyes would be filled with disgust. She had just killed someone. Not just someone, her best friend. She rubbed her stomach and swallowed back the bitter taste. She'd have to live with that choice for the rest of her days.

"I like red." Adelram brushed a hand through her hair, distracting her from her thoughts.

Her gaze flickered to his face. His expression made her heart soar. She reached for his hand, just as he reached for hers.

They limped out of the keep together. Past the knights. Past the burnt-out doorway. Past the still quiet lizard-birds. Past the black-skinned trees. Past the barren stretch of land. And into the edge of the Dryad's land.

"I need my necklace back."

His eyes dimmed and he swallowed. He took off the chain and handed it to her. "Why?"

Rennen smiled and led him to Shattered Oak. She dipped her bond necklace in her blood and in his and hung it on Shattered Oak's branch. It glittered in the sunlight with the rest of the promises.

"So, I can be your mate. Together we need to protect your people."

10

EPILOGUE: RENNEN

<u>Mid-morning, Luminous tenth, 300 years post-Merge</u>

150 year later...

The ground shook and the trees next to Rennin cracked from the wave of energy that pulsed from the cursed keep. The energy felt different and unnatural in a way she didn't understand. Something had changed.

She climbed the tree to her favorite spot to observe. Her perch had a view of the front gate. The gray stones still looked solid after all these years. The rusted portcullis was shut. She squinted at the replacement red door sealed years ago. The double doors that had not opened in a hundred and-fifty years creaked open.

Fear shot down her spine.

A cacophony of screeches and clanks sounded above her as a swarm of lizard-birds flew over her and descended on the keeps walls. The lizard-bird hadn't been seen or heard since they had sealed the keep. The additional ominous sign sent shivers down her spine.

The trapped evil within had broken the seal.

She had to tell the others and check on the Shattered Oak.

Time was of the essence. She jumped down and ran through the trees, taking the most direct route to the Oak. When she was close to the sacred grove, she stopped and walked, letting the peace of the area fill her. The soft tinkle of glass in the breeze added to the protected feeling.

Shattered Oak stood alone in the clearing. The glittering promises sparkled across the deep scar. The tree's healthy green leaves were a counterpoint to its deep scar. Despite everything Rennin and the other Tree Protectors had done over the years, the scar still remained. A sign that they had not vanquished the evil within.

Adelram's wolfish body pushed through the brush to her left. His pink tongue hung out and he rubbed against her in greeting. She'd been so lucky. The blessing of Shattered Oak had matched Adelram's life with her own. Gratitude and love swirled in her chest. She bent and hugged his furry form and stroked his thick, dark fur.

After a moment he transformed into his human form. "I heard the call."

She took his hand and leaned her forehead against the Matriarch's rough bark. The tree responded with a spark of recognition that started in her spine, "Seedling of the Dryad who saved me."

The tree's deep musky scent relaxed Rennen's shoulders. Shattered Oak would know what to do.

"Evil sought evil. As you must seek good. Go to New Nadezhda and seek the lighthouse for another guardian." The rustling sigh of Shattered Oak's leaves punctuated the tree's words. This was the most the tree had spoken. Even so, the message was not clear.

"I don't understand." An image of a city laid out below her filled her mind. The city was weeks to the west. She'd never seen a town as big as this one. Unease cramped her stomach. Was this really where she would get the help she needed?

"Seek Joshua Lighthouse." The tree's essence pulled away.

Her hand slid down the jagged bark from as high as she could reach to the top of the roots in ritual farewell. Her fingers broke contact.

"I can see you worrying." Adelram squeezed her hand gently. "Your mother and Zinnia can watch the land while we seek the new guardian."

"How are we going to find Joshua Lighthouse in a city this big?" Rennen realized that the tall structures in the middle were buildings and not big trees. There must have been hundreds of people if not more in the city in her vision.

"Shifters are everywhere. They will aid us." Adelram tugged her close. "Come my love. We will leave at dawn."

THE END

Congratulations on reaching the end of Rennen and Adelram's origin story! Stay tuned for a sneak peek of the first chapter in the first book of the Merged Series: "Book of Secrets" and meet Joshua Lighthouse.

Enjoy this book? You can make a big difference...

Reviews are the most powerful tools when it comes to getting notice for my books.

If you enjoyed this book, I'd be so grateful if you'd spend just five minutes leaving a review (as short as you like!).

Thank you very much.

Eager for exclusive content? Want to be the first to know about upcoming releases and get a free short story?

Sign up for Claudia Blood's Newsletter at https://dl.bookfunnel.com/u5nf3wa84m

You can unsubscribe at any time.

BOOK 1: BOOK OF SECRETS

Excerpt from Chapter 1: Joshua

<u>1AM, August 11, 2016 - Earth before the Merge</u>

Joshua Lighthouse's plan was simple. Sneak out the window, climb to the roof, and watch the meteor shower. Nothing was going to stop him.

Not even the strange heavy feeling which still hung in the air. The feeling of a storm coming. The forecast had been for clear skies, but he'd been unable to shake the feeling that something was coming. That something was wrong.

Every year the Perseid meteor shower came close to his birthday. This year the peak fell on his twelfth birthday and the peak of the meteor shower would happen at his birth hour and there was going to be an outburst. Double the normal number of meteors.

He tightened his hand around the backpack's handle hidden under his Star Wars bedspread. The details of his room were lost in the darkness. His new star projection clock didn't project enough light to chase away the dark shadows. Instead, it filled his bedroom with a steady clicking like the mandibles of a giant ant.

The digits on the clock took about a century to flip to two AM.

It was time.

He pulled out the remote control from the side pocket of his bag. A button turned on the camera on his spybot hidden on the top of his parent's wardrobe. The lever made the spybot crawl out from behind the discarded baseball caps, cups, and change. The camera focused on his parents in their king-sized bed.

His father's mouth opened wide, his arms flung out with one touching the nightstand and the other over part of his mom's pillow. His mom was hidden under the quilt with just the tips of her dark hair sticking out. Her arm hung over the side and twitched in time with father's snoring.

His parents were asleep.

The remote snapped back in place in his bag. He kicked off the covers. His toes sunk into the plush carpet as he crept across the room to open the window. The screen already sat hidden behind his dresser.

He scanned his neighborhood. The streetlight stood silent guard between dark houses.

He pulled out the second remote and sent Betty, his other little robot, from her hiding spot on the roof. She rolled to the edge and lowered the rope already around the chimney. It slithered down next to his window.

The climb took a moment. From his vantage point on the roof, the neighborhood spread out beneath him. The neighbor's black lab, Petey, lifted his head from his paws, snorted and curled back up in his kennel.

Joshua pulled up the rope, tucking it and the robot back in their hiding place. Fifteen steps brought him to the faint chalk X which marked the spot where the best view would be. In that spot, the chimney would block the light from downtown Rochester, and a gap in the trees would give him a wide view of the sky.

He sat on the spot and unpacked. Snacks – check. Binoculars around his neck – check, a blanket for his legs to ward off the chill – check.

Then he settled back on the roof. The trees in the backyard swayed gently in the slight breeze. The roof was rough and warm on his back. The faint smell of backyard fire hung in the air.

His eyes adjusted. The stars twinkled in swaths in the sky looking like spilled salt on his mom's black granite countertop. Lines traced the first passing meteors. Only the faint hum of mosquitoes and the flutter of a bat broke the quiet.

The Perseid meteor shower would go on for an hour. His parents were sound asleep so they'd never miss him. He'd be able to watch the whole thing.

Bong.

Bong.

The deep distant note of a gong tolled. He flinched and covered his ears, but it made no difference to the loudness of the noise.

The gong had a deeper tone than the bells of Assisi Heights up the hill. When the bells at Franciscan Sisters rang, his chest lightened. No, this was something different. That seed of worry that had been nagging him sprouted.

He tucked his blanket in his backpack and stood, walking towards the chimney, and braced his shoulder against it. His binoculars out, he scanned the horizon.

Nothing seemed amiss. The neighborhood lay quiet and

dark. Too quiet. Silence, so loud it echoed in his ears. The winds hid, the animals waited. But for what?

To the south, the pink and blue lights of downtown Rochester glowed. The feeling of a storm approaching deepened and his bones responded with an ache. He did a full circle scan, but saw nothing but cloudless, star speckled sky. Was he imagining it?

His eyes were drawn back to downtown, the stars behind the buildings disappeared. Not blocked by clouds, but gone, as if they had been drawn on an etch-a-sketch that a kid had shaken. The pit of his stomach gave another harder twist.

Dark splotches swarmed the Mayo building, army ants overrunning its prey. The darkness faded and left a gaping hole in the skyline. The building was gone.

The hairs on his body stood up as one. His heart drummed and he grabbed the chimney. The stone cut into his fingers.

The Plummer building floated up into the air, water and sparks trailed after it. What was he seeing? It made no sense. He pinched himself and the sharp pain made even less sense. He wasn't dreaming. But how could it be real?

<u>Wump-boom-ba-boom.</u>

The roof shook. His foot slipped from under him and only his hold on the chimney kept him upright. His heart skipped and he turned toward the sound.

A stone tower crushed the Miller's house next door, leaving Petey howling in his backyard kennel. Black spots swarmed the kennel fence and it disappeared. Petey tucked his tail and ran to the front of the house, yipping and whimpering.

From across the street, Mrs. Lake banged open her door. Petey huddled at her bare feet hiding his head under her checkered robe. She gaped at the new stone building, mouth wide, hand to her chest. She seemed about ready to faint.

At the bottom of her porch stairs, a single blue light grew until it looked like a swarm of fireflies. When they fizzled out, a skinny woman with a green-feathered body and long black feathers cresting from her head appeared. Her feathers fluffed up, making her seem bigger. Her long wailing cry broke the silence.

Mrs. Lake fell back against the door, clutching her blanket. She took one deep breath, her mouth hung open, eyes bulged.

Joshua leaned closer to the chimney. If Mrs. Lake looked ready to freak, then this was all real. He pushed down his fear and scanned again. Black swarms took things away, and blue light brought them. What made things move? The stone tower and the Plummer building had moved.

Another blue shimmer in the middle of the street and a large hedge appeared, blocking his view of Mrs. Lake and the green bird-lady. A deep fog rolled in ushering in the stench of rotten cabbage.

The fog made it easier to see faint orange lines which criss-crossed the street looking like a basket that was unraveling. Every third or fourth one brightened into a bolt of flickering orange lightning.

A faint hum brought his attention to an orange bolt inches away from the corner of his house. Stones and plants from the garden drifted up in the orange lightning. The orange lines must be what moved things. It thickened as he watched, embedding the orange bolt inside the edge of his house. If the lines caused movement that meant–.

The house beneath him shook and lifted, leaving the rest of the neighborhood, the hedge, and the fog all shrinking away. The orange light pulled his house higher and higher until every-thing on the ground was dollhouse sized. He was flying. A strange exhilaration gripped him.

Around him more and more orange bolts brightened, dragging along objects. The bolts were not straight, some turned and twisted around other bolts.

A grove of trees flew above him raining black dirt caught in another orange bolt. When they sped past, a worm landed on his shoulder. He jerked. The worm squirmed on his shoulder just before it fell. That woke him up. He was in danger, just like the worm.

<u>Bap-Bap-Bap</u>

The trees smacked like machine gun fire into a floating grey castle. The castle must've appeared like the bird lady and the fog. The trees splintered into chips and left cracks in the stone. A man in armor held onto the buttress which shook each time another tree hit. The castle sunk following its orange line down.

The air thickened with debris. The pops and bangs of a hundred such battles assaulted Joshua's ears. He felt a sting on his arm. He slapped it, and his hand came away bloody. He must've been hit by some broken glass.

Something pinged the roof sending a shingle flying. The house shook each time an object battered it. His house had stayed together, which wasn't what should've happened. Houses weren't meant to float and stay together, no matter what kid's movies might show.

He had no idea why, but so far buildings acted like ships on the sea and only when they crashed into something else, did they break. So far, his house hadn't been hit by anything big enough to break it apart.

The sharp tang of ozone and then a blue shimmer mid-air birthed a long wooden tower that pierced the air like a spear that punctured his house. A mortal wound, the house shuddered and pieces of Joshua's life fell away. His dresser, his train set, his clock plummeted. Where were his parents? He pulled out the monitor.

The video cameras he'd placed with such care showed

nothing but splinters and blood. The tower filled the whole floor. "Mom? Dad?" he whispered. His gut twisted like he had eaten that worm and all its brothers.

He wrapped his body around the chimney, cheek pressed against the brick. The feeling of displaced air made him look up. A pyramid, blotted out the sky and rushed toward him.

Adrenalin came online and pulsed through his system. His heart picked up speed.

Maybe if things came out of the blue light, he could use the light as a door to get out of here. He had no idea what was on the other side. It could be even worse. But he'd die for sure if he stayed here.

He focused on the blue light still at the far end of the towers that had pierced his family's home. He let go of the chimney and grabbed the rope attached to it, sliding down the way they did in the movies. Gravity no longer pulled just down. It pulled down at first and then shifted to the right causing him to slip and hit his shoulder on the house. The pain of hitting his shoulder blurred the edges of his vision.

If he didn't move, he'd be crushed.

He pulled hand over hand until he stood on the tower just outside his room. The tower had pierced his bed, obliterated his room.

The last of the tower pulled out of the blue light and the light shrank. The rope in his hand loosened. A brick from the chimney grazed his cheek.

He had one shot to run across the tower and leap into the blue light. If he missed before the light disappeared, he would fall to his death or be crushed.

The grinding of the rest of his house battling and losing against a stone pyramid faded as he focused on the ten paces between him and the end of the tower.

He stepped. His heart thumped a hundred times for each step.

His breath panted out.

On the tenth step, he leapt at the blue light now the size of a paper plate, diving like he would off the high board.

And fell.

Find out what happened to Joshua...

FROM THE AUTHOR

I love Dryads. I'd read a story about a dryad guardian. She had no idea how powerful she was, but she kicked-butt when her garden was attacked. I was enamored with the idea of a warrior dryad.

When I re-read this story a few years later, I realized that this could easily be in the Merged world. Then I got my first nibble of a story with Joshua Lighthouse.

Scales of the Dragon will be book 4 and should have Rennen, Adelram, Max, Joshua, and Alex.

And of course a dragon. :)

ACKNOWLEDGMENTS

Thanks to my hubby and family who allow me to wander away when I need to write.

To my VA Kelly I can't thank you enough for your undying enthusiasm and design sense. Social media is way less scary with you on my side.

To my amazing developmental editor Dawn Alexander who helped me organize my chaos and keep my inner achiever from getting too enthusiastic.

Thank you Fenley Grant for your amazing editing skills and for working me in when I am inevitably late.

Thank you Wendy for reading and giving feedback to my writing since college. (A scary number of years ago) You were always able to find a nugget of good that kept me going.

Thank you to the ladies at Lakehouse Writers group, Tammy, Val, MaryAnna, B, Jay, and Kim who have been a constant source of inspiration, motivation, and sanity checking.

Thank you to Val and MaryAnna who kept me honest on our accountability texts and for helping me figure out the end of this book. You both were so patient with my what-if-ing.

Thank you Antha and Christine for the many, many, many writing sprints. Without you guys I never would have gotten the book done.

Thank you to Calley for the daily checkins. Cookies!

ABOUT THE AUTHOR

Claudia Blood writes mystical realms and futuristic worlds, where underdogs defy authority, defeat demons, and discover their destined family amidst the chaos.

Her love of Epic Fantasies led her from life as a research scientist right into that of an award-winning author. With works such as the Renegades Rising, *Relic trilogy*, <u>Merged series</u>, and the <u>Supernatural Detective Agency</u>. Claudia Blood's works cover a wide range of genres and themes that have captivated many.

Juggling her roles as a wife, mom, business analyst, and pet wrangler doesn't leave much free time, but what Claudia has is filled to the brim with creating sci-fi and fantasy novels set in worlds that may be slightly familiar and some that are totally unique and new. Taking inspiration from all kinds of media from *Dungeons & Dragons*, *The Dresden Files*, Alan Dean Foster, and so much more, Claudia Blood crafts stories that entice and keep the reader wondering what will happen next.

For her latest release, visit her at
<u>www.ClaudiaBlood.com</u>

www.ingramcontent.com/pod-product-compliance
Lightning Source LLC
Chambersburg PA
CBHW071941210726
48293CB00004BA/1406